CROWN OF DEATH

Book One - Crown of Death Saga

KEARY TAYLOR

Taylor, Keary, 1987-
Crown of Death (Crown of Death) : a novel / by Keary Taylor. – 1st ed.

ALSO BY KEARY TAYLOR

~

THE HOUSE OF ROYALS SAGA

THE FALL OF ANGELS TRILOGY

THREE HEART ECHO

THE EDEN TRILOGY

THE McCAIN SAGA

WHAT I DIDN'T SAY

CHAPTER 1

RANDOM MUSCLE SPASMS CAN HAPPEN UP TO TWELVE HOURS after death.

I should have remembered that. This is what I do for a living, after all.

But I work on the body, in the basement of the funeral home, in the dark.

So when something suddenly pops me in the side as I take the dead man's socks off, a loud scream rips through my lips, echoing off the walls.

I whip around to see recently-deceased Paul Saundusky has smacked me in the ribcage as his muscles contracted one final time.

Skin and muscle tissue can continue to live for hours after death. And Mr. Paul has been dead for four of them.

"That wasn't nice, Mr. Paul," I say as my heart rate slowly relaxes toward a healthy rate. I shake my head as I return to his other sock, removing it. "Scaring a poor girl like that, all alone at work. It's late. You're the one who went and died, calling me into work after hours. You didn't have to be rude and go and freak me out, too."

I move on to his pants, slowly stripping the old man down.

"I bet you loved a good scare, didn't you?" I continue talking to the dead Mr. Paul over the sound of a new song playing from my speakers. "I bet you were always jumping out from around the corner at your poor wife. Or making ghostly sounds at your grandkids. You were a prankster, weren't you?"

Mr. Paul doesn't answer. None of them ever do, despite me talking to them, asking about their lives, telling them about mine.

They're dead.

Every one of them.

But somehow I enjoy their company.

"I know your type," I say as I finish undressing him. I move on to bathing and disinfecting his body. "My mom's dad was a little like you before he died. He was always teasing me and my little brother. He teased everyone. Especially girls, which let's face it, he probably shouldn't have been doing. He thought he was hilarious. Most of the time he was, but that man." I shake my head, wiping Mr. Paul's body down. "He could get a little sexist."

I bathe the dead man in water and chemicals. Killing off the germs that will only speed up the decomposing process.

On and on I talk, asking him about his wife. His kids. His grandkids.

I say he has five kids. Three girls, two boys. He only has four grandkids so far, because his youngest three kids are being stubborn about growing up and moving on with their lives.

"I'm sure they'll figure it out soon," I say as I wheel Mr. Paul over to the refrigerator and transfer him. "The traditional route isn't for all of us."

With a well wish goodnight, I slide Mr. Paul into the dark and close the door.

I sigh, looking over at the clock on the wall.

It's eleven o'clock. I officially got off work at three today, only Emmanuel, my boss and owner of Sykes Funeral Home, called me and told me we had a pick up. He'd gotten the body here with my help, then left to go enjoy the night with his wife and two kids.

Leaving me to start the grunt work.

I guess I am his apprentice, after all. If anyone around here is supposed to be the dead body grunt, it's me.

I lock up and step out into the fresh, non-formaldehyde-scented world. The late-June Colorado air is still warm. I climb into my car, start the engine, and head in the direction of home.

Greendale, a suburb outside of Denver, has been my home for the past two years. The community college was the only one in the area that had the program I wanted—Mortuary Science. I finished my associates just two months ago. I've been in apprenticeship at Sykes Funeral Home for a year, and have two more before I can take my licensing exam and strike out on my own.

The night is fairly quiet already as I drive just a few blocks to my apartment building. It's a run-down building, the kind where you don't look your neighbor in the eye for more than two seconds, and definitely the kind where you don't listen too hard to the conversations you hear through the too-thin walls.

But it's cheap, and the only two-bedroom place Amelia and I were able to afford.

All that's about to change, though.

I lock my car as I head up the stairs to the upper floor. I've read all those advice articles, the ones on how to protect yourself against predators. I already had my keys out and ready, so I immediately unlock the door and walk in.

The sounds of hissing, cooking food, and the fast-paced music of a dance party on the TV mix and assault my ears the moment I close the door behind me.

"Hey guys," I say with a surprised smile. "What, your TV not working?"

Amelia grunts an affirmative noise, and doesn't even look up at me, her gaze fixed on her movie. Her boyfriend, Tanner, has his arm around her. He absent-mindedly twists his finger around a lock of her hair.

I won't admit it out loud, but I'm happy to see them here. It's been awfully quiet the last two months. Amelia was my roommate for a little over a year. But two months ago she moved in with Tanner.

Now, it's usually just me in this rundown apartment.

My stomach immediately growls at the scent of food. I follow my nose toward the kitchen.

"You smell like dead people," Amelia says without looking away from the screen.

"You know you want to grind up all on this," I tease her, looking over my shoulder.

A little smile creeps onto her face, but she doesn't say anything.

I round the dining room, and the kitchen opens up.

Revealing Eli.

Cornelius Rath, or Eli, as I have always called him, takes the garlic from the cutting board and dumps it in the frying pan. He only glances up at me once as he goes back to his work, moving on to a salad in a big bowl.

"How was work?" he asks.

I give a little sigh, feeling myself relax.

Family. Someone I trust. Someone who's always here for me. Just the sound of his voice makes me feel calm. It's always so even. But, dark and wise.

Eli is a medium-toned man, with curly black hair, and black eyes. A single piercing holds a gold hoop in his left ear. Black, always, always black clothing hugs his toned body.

A single gold ring sits on the middle finger of his right hand, the crest of a raven set upon its surface.

"Fine," I say. "Pretty standard night. We'll finish preparing the body tomorrow, once the family knows how they'd like to proceed from here."

Eli nods, going back to the chicken, which from the smell of it, is nearly done.

My phone vibrates. Wondering who the hell is texting me this late, I reach into my back pocket and pull it out.

The name across the top—Shylock—sends my heart into my throat.

You haven't paid the next installment yet. Bring it tomorrow, or that pretty little roommate might look a little different the next time you see her.

Thud, thud, thud. My heart surges my blood through my body with hurricane strength.

Shit. Shit, shit, shit.

I'll get it to you tomorrow, I text back.

"What's wrong?"

My head whips up to find Eli studying me with narrowed, concerned eyes.

"Nothing," I lie, the word coming out a little too quick and panicked-sounding to be believable. "How was your day?" I squeeze into the kitchen behind him, washing my hands in the sink, even though I washed and disinfected them at work.

"Uneventful," he says as he continues his work, busying around the kitchen.

Be cool, I tell myself. *You've got the money. Amelia's not going to get hurt.*

I nod, drying my hands off. I wander back over to the table, a dated, round thing we picked off a curb with a piece of cardboard taped to it with FREE written in black marker.

I don't really understand what Eli does for a living. Something with security companies. Something with computers. Something that's during the day, a nine-to-five that must pay him fairly well.

"What are we eating tonight?" I ask. I lean back in my chair, kicking my feet up on another. I watch Eli as he works.

"Teriyaki chicken with a balsamic salad and jasmine rice," he explains. "I was going to make this earlier, but when I got here, Amelia said you'd been called in late."

"Thanks for waiting," I say.

He only makes an affirmative grunt.

I live in Greendale now, but I grew up in Cherico, the next town over, twenty minutes outside of Denver, my entire life. The same two-story brick house from the time I was a baby until I graduated high school two years ago.

When I was a freshman, Eli Rath moved into the cute, little white house across the street and down three houses.

To say he stood out was an understatement.

It was a family neighborhood, with kids and boring housewives and overworked dads. Eli was young, single, with a little bit of a dangerous edge to him.

But somehow he became a part of our family. He became friends with my parents. They'd stand out in the driveway talking for a long time, smiling and laughing politely. Soon he was invited over for family barbeques. Next it was Easter dinner, and by my senior year of high school, it was every holiday and most Sundays that he was in our house, like that was where he belonged.

And then I graduated. I moved here to Greendale for school, even though it's only thirty-five minutes from my parents' house.

Just a month into school, Eli had texted, telling me his office had moved here to Greendale, and he'd bought a new condo not too far from the school.

My best friend, the man who had always been there for me, for my family, was now only a few blocks from me at all times.

Over these past two years, he has always showed up once or twice a week with bags of food and an even smile on his lips. He'd cook for Amelia and me, and we'd spend the night chatting and laughing over dumb stories.

Eli looks over at me and I give him a little smile.

It's hard to classify Eli. Protective as a father. Wise as a grandfather. Loyal as a brother.

He's always been there for me.

I try to do the same. But I see it there. A little flicker of... something in his eyes.

Something a little dark. Something a little sad.

Something a little withdrawn.

But I've known Eli long enough now to know he'll never share whatever put that darkness in his eyes.

CHAPTER 2

"Hello?" I groggily say into my cell phone Friday morning. My eyes squinting against the bright light, I check the time. Five-freaking-twenty-one in the morning.

"Logan, I need you down here now," Emmanuel's voice cuts through the phone with an edge to it. "We got an...interesting one down here."

I groan and roll over onto my stomach. "Can't it wait until I'm supposed to come in at nine?"

"They're wanting to bury the poor woman tomorrow morning," he says. "And this one is going to take some... serious work."

I moan again and roll into a sitting position. "Fine," I say. "I'll be there in twenty."

Emmanuel doesn't even say anything else, just hangs up.

Rubbing my palms against my eyes, I stagger from my bed, into the bathroom.

Twenty-four minutes later, I unlock the doors and walk into the funeral home. Down the stairs I trudge, still hardly able to keep my eyes open. I hang my bag on the hook and pull on my lab coat.

"You said it'd be twenty minutes," Em growls as I push through the double doors. "That was five minutes ago."

"My alarm said it was supposed to be three hours from now," I say as I pull on some gloves. "We can't all get what we want."

I turn, and see the body that Emmanuel is trying to work on.

I say *trying*, because the poor woman is resting on the table in two pieces, the rest of her in ribbons.

"Holy hell," I breathe as I walk over, taking her in.

Her head has been torn from her body. It nearly looks like it was *bitten* off. The skin of her neck, though now gray and flat from loss of water, is torn and obviously ripped. The rest of her lies just below the head. She's covered from head to toe in bruises and scratches.

I see four indents and then long scratch marks. As if she were grabbed, tried to run, only the assailant didn't let go.

These marks are all over her body.

Her fingernails are broken and ragged, torn off.

"She fought hard," I say, taking her hand and holding it, looking at how some of them are broken clean off.

"Yes, she did," Em agrees, pausing, looking at this poor woman. "Every bit of her shows signs of beating. Like whoever did this played with her first. Like a cat and its prey."

"Have the police caught who did this?" I ask.

I've seen some pretty rough things down here in the basement of the mortuary. A lot of blood. Other bodily fluids. Gunshots. Rope burns around necks.

But even my stomach turns at the sight of this woman.

Emmanuel shakes his head. "Not yet. But the family is desperate to give her closure. To move on. Her body has been with the coroner for two weeks already. They just released it to me this morning. Family wants to bury her tomorrow."

"Open casket?" I ask in horror.

Emmanuel's gray eyes slide over to mine, and his own face a little pale, nods.

I let out a slow breath between my lips. I nod.

And we get to work.

Having to deal with Shylock and giving him most of my money was bad enough. And now this…

The news is filled with all kinds of horrible things that lead to dead people. Explosions. War. Mass shootings.

Sometimes you see pictures of bodies scattered about. Maybe all their parts aren't still connected to them. Your stomach turns. You say a little prayer.

Your life moves on.

Those bodies move on, too.

To people like Emmanuel and myself.

We do the best we can to put them back together. To make them look like they once did. So that those loved ones still here in this life can move on.

One square inch of her at a time, we move. Stitching up. Using wax to close over parts of her that cannot be pieced together. We use *tubes* of makeup. Carefully, so carefully not to pull any of it out, because it's been so much time, we brush her hair and carefully arrange it.

We return her head atop her shoulders. For hours we work on making it look like there aren't huge chunks of flesh missing. We cover it all up.

"Who would do this?" I say in a whisper. Half to Emmanuel. Half to this woman. As if she could answer me and tell me the horrific truths of what she saw in her final moments.

"A monster, that's who," Emmanuel says as he gently dresses her in the clothing the family provided.

I shake my head. Someone capable of this level of violence doesn't deserve to be called human, anymore.

It takes the entire day, but by the time dinner rolls around, Miss Carolina Jex looks ready. Her face looks somewhat fake, worked over with so many layers of makeup. But she doesn't look like a chopped-up cadaver. I think the family will be able to get what they need from this open casket funeral.

"You did good, Logan," Emmanuel says as we take our gloves off and wash death down the drain. "I'll call in Craig and Katie to help with the service. You've put in more than enough hours this week."

"Are you sure?" I ask, rolling my head from one side to the other, trying to stretch out the kinks and knots that have formed throughout the day.

Emmanuel nods, and I place a hand on his forearm. "Thanks. You're a good man, Em."

He offers a thin little smile and nods. "Get some rest, Logan. I'll finish up here."

I look once more at Carolina, now resting peacefully in the casket. "Goodnight."

Some days this feels like any other job. I forget that my work is based upon when people die. To me it's no different than a waiter at a restaurant, or a schoolteacher.

But there are days like today, when I walk out into the bright, sunny day, absolutely disoriented and dazed that the sun could possibly be shining, that I am reminded.

We all die eventually. Everyone's paths to get to that gate are entirely different.

I pray that my arrival will be peaceful.

But, considering my luck, there's not a chance.

Just as I sink into the driver's seat of my car, my phone vibrates. I look down to see a text from my little brother, Eshan.

Mom is making tortellini. Eli just got here. Wanna join?

I keep staring at my phone. Really I just want to curl up in my too-small bathtub, turn off the lights, and not think about anything until the water goes cold.

But it's Eshan, and Eli, and my parents who I haven't called or seen in three weeks.

So with exhausted fingers, I text my brother back. *Be there in twenty.*

The traffic is moderate as I work my way from one town to another. I don't cut through the city, which would be awful this time of day, but take the longer route around the outskirts. Past businesses and homes. Through the normal.

Regular life rolls on no matter how horrible things might have been around them. Oblivious and blessed for it.

I turn onto my old street and roll past Eli's old house. And then there's my parents' red brick house. I park along the curb behind Eli's black car and walk up to the door.

Everyone's laughter hits my ears as I walk inside. The front room is calm and put together, as always. I walk past the stairs and into the dining room.

Eli sits at the table with Eshan and my father wheels around the kitchen, attempting to help my mother with dinner in the kitchen.

"Hey, sweetie," Mom says with a warm smile when I plop down at the table next to Eli. "Dinner will be done in just a minute."

I smile, though I can tell it doesn't reach my eyes.

"You smell like dead people," Eshan says, a little devil's look in his eyes as he smiles.

This is normally our thing. Teasing each other. Getting on each other's backs about everything.

But I just don't have it in me today.

So I don't say anything. I just look away, watching my parents without really seeing them.

"Are you alright?" Eli asks.

I shrug, not looking at him so he can't read the weight of the day written across my face.

"Food is ready!" Dad declares. He pulls a few dishes into his lap and wheels his chair over, mom brings the rest, and they set it on the table. We all gather round, one big, mismatched, happy family.

My father, Ethan Pierce, has strawberry blond hair that is slowly thinning, to where he'll have to start shaving it soon. But, he's thick and strong. Though he doesn't feel it right now while he's stuck in that wheelchair. He's been building custom homes since long before I was born.

My mom, Gemma Pierce, is beautiful. With blonde hair that toes the line into platinum—and it's her natural color—blue eyes, petite figure, she's a bombshell. She's kind and warm, but is also always worried about what other people think of her outside of the house. But at home, she's just mom to me and my brother.

Then there's me. Dark brown hair. Light hazel eyes that I've been told more than once look kind of like a cat's. I'm a little shorter and my lips are fuller and round.

And Eshan. With his lanky build and dark chestnut skin. Big brown eyes and perfectly smooth complexion.

And Eli. Black eyes, black hair, black skin.

None of us are family by blood, but family through the heart.

I was placed in Ethan and Gemma's home as a three-day-old baby. They'd never been able to have children of their own. And then when I was five, my parents brought Eshan home from Nepal, one year old. And then there was Eli, who didn't quite fit the role of brother, son, or uncle. But, he found a place, nevertheless.

They all chat and laugh, and normally I'd be laughing the loudest of them all, making some brash joke. But I keep thinking about poor Carolina today and the impossible state she was brought to us in.

"Logan," Dad says, pausing with his spoon over his bowl. "You've been near dead silent all night. What's wrong?"

I feel all eyes land on me and my face heats. I've never been one to hold much back.

"Just work," I say, shrugging. "There was this poor woman. It was…"

"No gruesome details at the dinner table," Mom cuts in, her face already turning pale. She's never handled my chosen profession well.

"It was bad," I say instead with a nod. "It was just hard, seeing that someone so seemingly normal could be treated so violently."

No one says anything for a moment, because what is there really to say?

"I can't even imagine the things you have to deal with sometimes," Dad says, giving me a sympathetic look.

Dad fell off some scaffolding four months ago. He broke his back.

Broke it.

Somehow, he isn't paralyzed. He's just slowly having to relearn how to walk.

But there was a time, when the bills were pilling in, and the money had stopped. And my family needed help.

So, even further into debt with Shylock I went.

And now I get threats, my friends get threats, my family gets threats.

So I get terrifying encounters, making payments so he doesn't hurt anyone.

I shrug and look over to my brother, who has this little

look in his eyes that tells me he wants the gory details of work later.

Eli has something in his eyes too, but I can't quite peg it down.

The family moves to the living room after dinner and strikes up a game of Mexican Train. I play, though not well.

And Eli sits on the couch, tapping something into his phone and reading. His work spills into personal hours occasionally.

By nine o'clock I'm exhausted from the early start to the day and the emotionally draining work. I say goodnight to my family and Eli and I head outside.

"It must have been pretty awful," Eli says as we slowly walk down the sidewalk. We pause at the curb, next to our cars. "You've dealt with some pretty gruesome stuff, but normally nothing gets to you. Not like this."

I wrap my arms around myself, even though it isn't cold. I shake my head as my eyes wander down the street I know so well. "It was awful. I mean, this woman's head was ripped —and I mean *ripped*—from her body. It looked like…I don't know, it'd been clawed off, or chewed on. And every bit of her was bruised and beaten. It was just so…inhumane."

My eyes drift back to Eli's. And that darkness that always resides in them, it grows a little more black. A little deeper.

"How long ago was she killed?" he asks. And something in his voice sounds tight.

I slide my hands into my back pockets. "Over two weeks ago. And the family wanted an open casket. I've…I've never had to do so much work on a body."

Eli remains quiet, which isn't unusual. He isn't the most talkative person. But it feels weighted. Contemplative. I look into his face, trying to decipher what he's thinking.

And he realizes I'm watching him. He blinks twice, his eyes coming back into focus. "I'm sorry today was so hard for you, Logan. It sounds like you could use some sleep."

I nod, indeed feeling incredibly tired, like I could sleep from now until noon tomorrow. "Yeah," I say.

"I'll meet you at your place tomorrow for our run?" he asks as he backs toward his car.

"See you tomorrow," I say.

Eli tries to give me a little smile before he slips into his car, but it's tiny, and absolutely forced. He shuts the car door, starts the engine.

And tears off into the darkening evening, wheels spinning on the concrete.

CHAPTER 3

I WATCH THE CITY MOVE ALONG, THOUGH IT'S STILL SLEEPY on a Saturday at eight in the morning. A van full of kids drives by, the windows down. Noise spills out, a shrill scream from a baby cuts through the day. A couple on a bicycle speeds by, dressed in full gear. The coffee shop across the street only has a few caffeine-fueled customers at this point.

In my running gear, I wait, leaning against my car, watching for Eli.

It's been a tradition ever since he moved so close in Greendale. Eli is ripped and in incredible physical shape. Maybe he stays so fit because of his job, I don't really know. But he likes to run. And I started running with him. So, every Saturday morning for the past nearly two years, we go running.

He's always harping on me about staying in good physical shape. Once I got over myself and realized he wasn't trying to call me fat, I came to see that he was saying it because he's always been a little over-protective. He is the one, after all, who has told me how to protect myself from parking lot predators. The one who has showed me how to flip a grown man over my shoulder. Who showed me all the right places to strike if anyone came after me.

The black car rounds into the parking lot and I stand, watching as Eli climbs out of it.

He wears a tight black athletic t-shirt and track pants. Every bit of it highlights his toned physique.

But the second I meet his eyes, I know that something's off.

"Ready?" he asks without a friendly word of greeting. He just nods his head down the road, down our usual path.

"Uh, yeah," I stumble through words. I scramble to my feet and follow after him. We cross the parking lot, and round to the sidewalk that cuts through the main part of town.

"I did some research about the woman you told me about last night," he immediately says as soon as we start jogging. I look over at him, my brows furrowed. He only stares forward with intense eyes. "The police found her just a block from here."

My stomach flops, and rolls over, and at the same time my heart decides to try a little backflip. "Are you serious?"

Eli nods. "Just one block in the other direction. Between your apartment and your work. The police found her body, but no traces of who did that to her. They first suspected it might be an animal attack."

"But those bruise and scratch marks," I say, the sight of

her black and blue flesh flashing across my vision. "Those were made by human hands."

Eli nods once more. "The police haven't found any leads as to who did this. No suspects. For as much damage as they did, they left very little evidence."

I shake my head, huffing a bit as my heart rate increases and my lungs have to work a little harder. "So this person is still running around?"

"Two nights ago, another woman was attacked," Eli says, and now he does give a little look in my direction. "On the other side of Greendale."

My step falters, and I catch myself before I trip. Eli slows, looking back at me, but we continue jogging.

"Same injuries?" I question, fearful of what the answer might be.

He nods. "The victim was decapitated. Covered in bruises. Body heavily damaged."

"Here, in Greendale?" I gape.

"Yes," Eli says. His breathing is hardly labored, even though he's talking. "Again, police have no idea who did it. They're getting worried this is a serial killer."

I swear through my heavy breathing.

That's terrifying. A serial killer, right here in my town.

Suddenly, Eli slows, and I blast past him for five steps before I realize. I stop, looking back at him, and see him standing in the middle of the sidewalk.

"I think you should move back home with your parents," Eli says.

And despite how ridiculous his statement just was, the look on his face is dead serious.

"The first victim was found less than three hundred yards from your home," Eli says, steeling his look, because he knows how I'm going to react in just a minute. "He's obviously targeting women, women who were alone. And he seems to have taken a liking to Greendale."

"So your solution is that I just pick up and *move*?" I say, my tone quickly transitioning over to mocking. "That I just tell my boss, 'sorry, this is too scary. I'm going to run home to the protective arms of mommy and daddy'?" I give a huff of a laugh. "That's ridiculous, Eli."

His gaze doesn't soften. Doesn't show any signs that he's kidding. "You saw that woman, Logan. You saw what this person is capable of. Would you risk that the next body in the basement of your funeral home is your own?"

I take a step forward and feel my blood turn hot. "Oh my... You're... You're serious about this. That because two women were killed-"

"Yes, *killed*, Logan," he interrupts me. "Brutally."

"That I just uproot everything." I look at him in annoyance. I shake my head. "How much of a dainty, defenseless girl do you think I am?"

"It is not about that Logan. I-"

"I...I can't believe you're being serious about this," I say, looking sideways at him, my brows furrowed. "Don't you think you're over-reacting just a little?"

"No," he says, his face stone still. "I really don't."

I huff another disbelieving laugh. And I step forward, past him, back in the direction of home.

"Logan," he says, following after me. "I know it seems a little extreme, but trust me, I've seen situations like this before with my work. And the very last person you expect could be this psycho's next victim. I won't risk that the next woman to lose her head might be you."

I look to the side, glaring at him as he quickly follows me. "I don't know who the hell you think you are that you can just tell me to change my life at the snap of your paranoid fingers, Eli."

Like I slapped him in the face, he stops, looking at me through slit eyes.

"I'm…" he stammers for a moment. Something Eli never does. "I'm your friend, Logan. I'm just looking out for you."

"That's not actually your job, Eli," I say. I fix my eyes on the sidewalk in front of me, refusing to look at him. "You're not my father. You're not my brother. You're certainly not my boyfriend. So keep your nose in your own damn business."

"Logan," he says, his tone growing a little more desperate. "This is a dangerous situation. You can nearly *see* the alley where the woman was killed from your dining room window! Please, just consider this."

We round into the parking lot of my building. And I stop suddenly, turning on him. "I think you need to go home, Eli. I am a grown-ass woman, and I decide what is best for me. Not you!"

I'm huffing, like I just ran three miles. My hands are on

my hips, and I look around, anywhere but at Eli, because my insides are all twisted scrap metal.

I've never felt so betrayed. So hurt.

And from someone who matters so much.

"Logan," he says, his voice a little breathy and taken off guard. "I…" But he doesn't complete the sentence.

"I'm *not* leaving," I say, finally meeting his eyes, and I hope he can see in them that I'm serious. And mad. "You should go home, and I don't want to see you for a while."

And I walk away.

Maybe I'm being overly dramatic. Maybe I'm over-reacting.

But that hurt. Him trying to tell me what to do. Eli assuming I couldn't take care of myself.

I climb the stairs, aiming for my door.

I halt in front of it, taking in the bright pink piece of paper taped to the door.

EVICTION NOTICE.

And I'm just done with this day.

"I'M TELLING YOU," AMELIA SAYS AS SHE DIPS HER FRENCH fry in my Butterfinger shake, "It's all that sexual tension. You two just need to bang it out and then everything can go back to normal."

"You have no idea how disgusting that suggestion really is," I cringe. I scoop a huge spoonful of the shake and stick it in my mouth. "I mean, Eli is family. You might have had a thing for him, but the suggestion of me and him..."

Internally, I actually gag.

Not that Eli isn't a good-looking man with a killer body. But still...family.

I cock an eyebrow and nod as I swallow the giant bite down.

"Well at some point there's got to be a man who comes along and gets you all hot and bothered," Amelia says as she shakes her head and dips another fry. "This has been torture, now that I have Tanner, and you're just always the third wheel. Find a man, Lo!"

"Hey, you asshole!" I bite back, wielding my spoon in her direction. "I may not just walk up to some kid in class and tell him I think he's hot, but-"

"But perhaps you should!" she says, teasing me. "Then you could finally get rid of some of that pent-up bitterness. Just be bold! Tanner and me were making out two hours later, and now look at us. A year later and we're talking about-"

She suddenly cuts off, like she's said more than she meant to.

"What?" I prod. She blushes hard, and bites her lower lip. "Oh, come on. You can't just lead into that and not finish the sentence."

She gives me a little wary smile, looking up at me from under her eyelashes. "We're talking about...if we might get married someday."

"What?" I gape. I actually fling my spoon in a big arc, sending a splatter of ice cream onto the window beside me.

"Married? Slow down on me, Amelia. You two just moved in together. Is this for real?"

She blushes harder and tucks a lock of hair behind her ear. "Yeah," she says. "I mean, we're all in this. I don't know a timeframe, but I feel like this is the right move."

I study her. My best friend ever since I started at Greendale Community College. My five foot-nine, blonde babe best friend with the pouty lips and the green eyes of a siren.

Talking about getting married.

"Wow," I breathe. "Amelia, that's amazing. I'm…I'm really happy for you."

"Really?" she asks, sounding wary. The look in her eyes tells me how much she's been dreading telling me. "You really mean it?"

I laugh, reaching forward and grabbing her hands. "Just because I have the worst luck in the world and can't seem to ever catch a break in the happiness department doesn't mean you're doomed, too. You and Tanner are great together. He worships the ground you walk on. Trust me, he recognizes that you're out of his league."

She laughs at that, smiling brightly.

"And even though you've already abandoned me in that apartment," I say, gazing at her through my laugh. "I'm happy for you. You have my full support."

I'll never tell her that because she moved out, because of my debt to Shylock, I can no longer afford the rent on my own. That I'm getting kicked out. That the eviction notice on my door said I had to be out in two weeks.

She doesn't need that guilt on her mind.

She does this relieved groan, leaning forward and kissing my cheek. "This is why you're the best, Lo. Thank you, thank you!"

I laugh, shaking my head.

She launches back into the shenanigans of her life, telling me about her upcoming semester this fall, continuing in her pursuit of going into human resources. And eventually, she turns to teasing me about wanting to work with dead bodies for the rest of my life.

We finish dinner around nine and Tanner texts her, asking her which of two movies she wants to rent that night.

"Do you want to come over?" she asks. "I promise we'll keep our hands to ourselves."

I shake my head with a laugh. "Go. Enjoy your boy toy. I'm beat. I think I'm just going to go to bed early."

"Fine," she says. With a kiss to my cheek, she says goodbye and heads to her car.

So, alone, I hop in my own, and head back home, feeling like a loner for being on my own on a Saturday night, heading home early.

I park and climb out.

And I slow as I approach the stairs up to my apartment.

Sitting on the bottom one, is Eli.

An exasperated sigh slips between my lips. "What are you doing here?"

He stands, his dark eyes fixed on me as he does. "I came to apologize for the way I acted before. And to…talk.

We stand there in the darkening light, in the parking lot of my seedy apartment building. Staring each other down, I can just see it there in his eyes. He doesn't actually regret anything he said to me earlier.

"I'm not moving," I say, folding my arms over my chest.

Though suddenly I realize—I am about to be homeless. I can't afford next month's rent, there's no way I can back-pay what I owe. Moving back home really might be my only option right now.

Not that I'm going to breathe a word of that to Eli.

"I'm sorry for how I presented it to you before," he says, standing tall and rigid. "I should have been better with my reasoning and presentation. I didn't mean to upset you."

I just stare at him, because he's making it very obvious that he doesn't think the heart of what he was saying was wrong.

"Can we go inside?" he asks, his eyes drifting up to the second floor.

My fingers curl into fists. Heat rises in my veins.

Because if he's requesting we go inside, he must think there's going to be a scene.

"I think we're good out here," I say.

I'm angry. On edge. Ready to throw verbal punches if I have to. Even if Eli is one of my best friends. Even if he is family.

"Okay, then," he says with a little nod. "But can you just try to see that I only said what I did because I care about you?"

"Sure," I say. My blood is growing so hot. "You can care about me. But expecting me to just pick up my life and move, is a little over the top, don't you think?"

"No, Logan," he growls, his tone rising. "I don't. You might be an adult, might be working your dream job, might be living on your own, but you don't know everything like you sometimes seem to think."

"Are you trying to sound like a condescending asshole?" I seethe, my tone rising. "Because you're doing a pretty damn good job, Eli!"

A scream cuts through the night.

Piercing.

Loud.

Utterly terrified.

And I look toward the street, just in time to see…something.

A motion.

A blur.

One figure. And then another.

"No," Eli breathes.

And I see every muscle in his body tighten. Constrict. Prepare.

"Get inside," he says.

The entire moment plays out in slow motion.

His eyes slide back to mine. Filled with terror. Filled with fight.

And for just a fraction of a second, I swear I see the faintest flecks of yellow in his dark eyes.

"Get inside, Logan," he says as a second scream pierces the night.

And then he's running.

Through the parking lot. Around the corner.

And despite how utterly pissed off I am with him right now, I still chase after him into the night.

Another scream rips through the night, only it's cut off.

I race past the vape shop. Around the gas station.

And there ahead, between an apartment building and a Mexican grocery store, I see Eli slip into the darkness. He hides in the shadows, watching.

And there's yelling.

Shouts.

A cry—not a scream.

And a roar.

Something inhuman. It reverberates off the walls.

I step into view of the dark, narrow space in time to see brilliant red glowing eyes fix on me.

A man, tall, muscular, backs away from two other figures, leaving a motionless female figure lying at his feet.

"You've had your fun these past two months, Rhys," a female voice says. "But you know how the Houses and Court feel about exposure."

The man with the glowing eyes laughs. "You and your Houses. Don't you ever get tired of being on the leash? Don't you ever get tired of holding it, Edmond?"

"I don't know," a male voice says. "Don't you think it suits me?"

Rhys laughs again. And I don't even see it, have no idea how he does it, but suddenly he lunges at a wall. He uses his momentum, kicking off the brick. He launches over the two figures.

He clears the alley, into the street.

Just fifteen feet from me, where I stupidly stand on the sidewalk, gaping.

His glowing red eyes lock on me. And I'm frozen as he lunges forward.

A thick set of arms wrap around him, and the two figures collide in mid-air, tumbling over the concrete.

Eli tackles the man, turning over, rolling.

A scream rips from my throat and I dart forward two steps.

But before I can get within ten feet, the two figures from the alley explode from it.

I don't know what happened.

One second Eli was wrestling Rhys.

The next a head is rolling down the road, the man and the woman panting, looking at Eli and me with equally brilliant red eyes.

CHAPTER 4

ELI SWEARS.

I don't think I've ever heard him swear before. But he does. Loud and blunt.

"You've both seen an awful lot in the last sixty seconds," the man says, looking up from Eli to me from beneath his dark eyelashes. "And for some reason you seemed to think you could do something about our little scene." He directs his words at Eli. "Why?"

Eli slowly rises to his feet. He holds his hands out slightly, as if to hold the two of them back. That's fear in his eyes. Genuine fear.

Justified. Considering the decapitated man lying in the street. The lifeless woman resting in the alley behind us.

What... Oh, lord. What...what is happening?

Why are their eyes glowing like that?

How did they move like they did?

"I just heard a woman scream," Eli says as he takes a slow step sideways toward my side. "I came to help. We...we didn't see anything. I swear. We'll go."

The woman laughs and my blood chills.

We've just been witness to...to what? We watched them kill that man. And that woman he killed...

The man before us narrows his eyes at me. He takes two steps forward, searching my face. "What's your name?" he asks. His voice is smooth like butter, and carries a faint Spanish accent.

My mouth opens just slightly to answer, but no sound comes out.

"She's no one," Eli interjects before I can even answer. "I promise, we'll cause you no trouble. Just let us go and you'll never hear a word from us."

"I'm afraid this is a bit of a problem for us," the woman says, taking a step forward.

My heart rate doubles. Sweat breaks out onto my palms. Fear crawls through me like a million ants.

"No," the man says, taking two more steps forward through the darkening night. "I know you. Don't lie to me. What House are you affiliated with? Sidra? Martials?"

"Hou...house?" I stammer, looking from him, to Eli. "I... I don't know what you're talking about."

The man's eyes flare brighter, red and brilliant.

A hiss rips from his lips and he becomes a blur. And then he's in my face.

Fangs, pointed, glistening *fangs* in my face, he growls,

grabbing the front of my shirt, pulling me an inch from his own face.

"Tell me your name," he growls.

Eli leaps at us, only the woman plows into him, knocking them both to the ground. He's swinging, wrestling, roaring. "We're no one," he bellows. "Release us and I swear on my life we will cause you no trouble."

"Why did you follow us?" the man hisses into my face. "Who are you spying for?"

"I'm not a spy," I say. A lick of anger flares in my blood. I shake my head, my entire body shaking violently. "I swear. We're just in the wrong place at the wrong time."

His eyes harden, and he suddenly steps away, but his hand latches around my wrist, and he yanks me forward. I stumble, nearly tripping. I cry out in pain as his hand tightens around my wrist. Like steel clamps.

"No," Eli yells. "Please. You don't have to do this."

The woman yanks him forward. She's surprisingly strong, because as he tries to yank out of her grasp, she wrenches his hands behind his back, twisting him into a painful hold he can't seem to break.

The war inside of me, of emotions swinging between terror and raging anger, is very real. "Please," I plead, fear reaching frantic levels in my blood. Anger and confusion make my vision blur. "I swear, we won't say anything. Just let us *go!*"

Neither the man nor the woman say anything as they march us down the road.

I debate screaming. Letting a blood curdling scream rip from my lungs, calling for help.

But I look over to Eli, and see that the woman holds a blade in her hand, wedged into his side.

Two blocks we trek, and then we turn into a door. It's a big steel one, industrial.

There are no lights on in the building. It smells strongly of gasoline and rubber.

My captor unlocks the door and shoves me into the dark.

I'm going to die. This is where they will kill us.

Pitch dark swallows me as I'm shoved inside, stumbling over a hard floor. The sound of keys echo once more, and I hear a heavy lock sliding into place.

Eli's shoulder bumps into mine in the dark. He continues pleading for our release, but is only met with silence.

Hands grip me once more and I hear the clanging of chains against metal and then a snap.

I'm shoved down and I fall into a seat. The next moment my wrists are yanked back, and a chain is looped around my wrists and something clicks into place.

I'm a prisoner. Locked up. About to die in the dark.

Yep. This is just my luck.

I should have gone with Amelia to Tanner's and watched that movie with them.

I should have gone with Eli into my apartment to talk.

Any number of paths that would have led to a different outcome than the one where I am about to die.

There's the sound of a match being struck and then a candle casts dim light.

Cinderblock walls surround us, all the way up to the ceiling, maybe twenty feet above our heads. A garage door is half bricked up, and a single steel door marks where we entered.

My guess is that it was once an auto-body shop.

The man steps back into view, walking toward me. He bends over, bracing his hands on his knees, looking me in the eye.

"Who are you, and who are you working for?" he says, his voice calm and even.

"We're no one!" Eli demands again. He's growing more frantic by the moment.

I look at my captor. He's in his mid-to upper-twenties, I'd guess. His complexion is a little darker. Black hair sits atop his head, messy, but purposeful. Dark, dark brown, nearly black eyes have taken over the glowing red. He's cut, in incredible shape beneath those jeans and that black t-shirt.

"I know I've seen you before," he says again, his voice even but dangerous. "Tell me your name."

"My name is Logan Pierce," I blurt, my voice trembling. "I've lived in this area my entire life. And I can say without a doubt that we have never, ever met before."

His jaw clenches and his eyes grow harder as he presses his lips together. He straightens and stalks over to the chair where Eli is chained, his wrists fastened to the arms of the chair, his ankles shackled, as well.

"You're certainly more capable than you smell," he says, placing his hands on the arms of Eli's chair, leaning down and studying him. "What are you? A hunter? Were you following us? Looking to take us out?"

"I have no weapons on me," Eli says, his voice evening out just a little.

"Oh, but that's a lie," the woman says, stepping forward. In her hand, she holds a pointed bit of wood, maybe ten inches long. "I pulled this from the waist of your pants."

My eyes widen, and flick back to Eli.

The look on his face tells me she isn't lying.

"Eli?" I breathe, immediately realizing my fatal mistake in giving away at least his first name. "Do you...do you know what's happening? Why would you be carrying a stake?"

He won't look at me. He only stares the man down.

The man hisses. His eyes drift down, studying Eli. And he goes still as his eyes fix on Eli's hand.

And the ring that rests on his middle finger.

"Conrath," the man growls as he grabs Eli's hand and yanks it toward him, the chains clanking. "You little liar."

He looks over at me and studies my face again. Deeply. Searching.

My eyes. My nose. My mouth. My jaw.

He's taking in every single detail of me, memorizing my features.

And slowly, slowly, a wicked smile grows on his lips.

"No," Eli says. "No! She has nothing to do with anything. She's nothing more than my friend. She has nothing to do with the Houses."

"Oh, you are such a liar," the man says. He releases Eli's

hand and stands straight. He reaches into his pocket and pulls out a cell phone.

"She's no one," Eli growls, growing angrier and more desperate by the moment.

"A guardian from the House of Conrath and a face that looks so achingly familiar?" the man says as he dials a phone number and then holds it up to his ear. "I don't think so. You know what I think? That Court will be very, very interested to get a phone call from the House of Valdez."

He goes quiet and listens for a moment. He turns his back to us and slowly walks toward the other side of the space as he talks quietly.

"What's going on, Eli?" I breathe through my quivering lips. I'm shivering violently. "What is he talking about? Why the hell are you carrying a stake? Who is he calling? What does Conrath mean?"

At the word Conrath, Eli noticeably flinches. His jaw tightens.

But he doesn't look at me. His eyes remain fixed on the man in the corner, quietly talking into the phone.

"He is wearing the Conrath crest," he quietly says. "I'm telling you, she looks just like her."

He's quiet, listening.

"Who does he think I am?" I ask, starting to feel frantic. "I look like who?"

"Quiet," Eli finally says, a little bark to his voice.

"I understand that doesn't mean she's anything but human, but I'm asking you to consider the fact that this man is here *guarding* her," our captor says. "That has to mean something. And considering it's the House of Conrath? From what I hear, he and their leader have some…interesting history."

Eli's breathing grows heavier.

I look over at him. And I consider.

Guardian.

That's what the man said Eli was to me.

Guardian.

Have I ever been more than just a few minutes away from Eli? Was it merely coincidence that he moved in just a few doors down? That he moved to Greendale as soon as I did? That he is *always* around?

"Eli?" I breathe. But I can't bring myself to ask the question. *Did you plant yourself in my life for a hidden reason?*

"Thank you," the man says, sounding absolutely relieved.

Eli's breathing is ragged. He leans forward, his fingers curling around the arms of the chair. His knuckles turn white.

"I said move back in with your parents," he says. I've never heard his voice sound like that. So low. So utterly dangerous. "I should have taken immediate action. Now all these years may be for *nothing.*"

My heart beats as a dull thud in my chest. The rest of me is as numb and dead as the bodies on my table as I try to make sense of his words.

The man in the corner suddenly stands ramrod straight, every muscle in his body pulled tight. He presses the phone a little harder to his ear, listening.

"No," Eli growls once more. "She is no one. She is *nothing* to the Court. Let her go!"

The man is quiet for a beat longer. And then he slowly turns back toward us, his eyes locking straight on Eli's.

"He says to ask you how many years it has been since a measly Bitten beat him to killing Henry," the man says. "Rath?"

And a purely animal roar bellows from Eli as he jerks forward. The bolts securing the chair to the concrete floor groan, threatening to snap.

And now I know I don't imagine it. For just a moment, there is a ripple of yellow that washes through Eli's eyes.

The man chuckles. "Oh, it's him."

He listens again, and the man's eyes snap over to my face. "I'm certain. She has to be."

I can hardly breathe. Darkness flickers all around the edges of my vision. I'm breathing too fast. There's too much panic and adrenaline surging through my veins.

I'm going to pass out.

I'm going to faint.

"I understand," the man says. "We shall see you in twelve hours."

Another unearthly roar rips from Eli.

The man ends the call, sliding the phone into his back pocket. Eli bellows and roars like a tied, starved lion, fighting against his bonds. I hear one of the bolts snap.

"This is about to get very, very interesting," the man says. And from his pocket, he produces something. Before I can identify it, he jabs it into the side of Eli's neck. He immediately slumps still.

A scream rips from my lungs and I try to lunge to him, only I just rattle my chains.

"I promise you he is not dead," the man says, tossing the syringe into a corner. I hear glass shatter. "But he had to be contained before he caused me a problem. He'll wake near morning."

He'll wake. Meaning this man doesn't plan to kill him before then.

"Who are you?" my voice quakes, but comes out clear and strong. "Why are you doing this?"

I jump at the sound of metal scraping concrete. He drags a metal chair across the floor. He sets it just in front of me and sits, resting his elbows on his knees.

"My name is Edmond Valdez," he says, his voice beautiful and luring. "I am one of the heirs to the House of Valdez." He studies me once more, but instead of the smirk and scheming in his eyes, I just see searching. "I'm doing this because you look exactly like your mother, and that makes you very, very interesting to the Court."

"My…my mother?" I question, confused at the turn this has taken. "I…I don't look anything like her. I'm…I'm adopted."

Understanding dawns in his eyes, and a little smile pulls at the corner of his mouth. "Ah. That makes sense, then."

I shake my head, blinking three times fast. "No. None… none of this makes sense."

He smiles sympathetically. "It will soon. All of this is because you look so very much like your *birth* mother. I'd question if I'm just seeing things. But *his* presence," he nods his head at Eli, "just confirms it."

"My birth mother?" I question. "You…how could you possibly know who she is? It was a closed adoption. My parents don't even know her name."

Edmond smiles, and I think that really is genuine pity in his eyes. "Because I've met the woman, on more than one occasion. She was at my House just two years ago. You have her same nose, lips, brow. Your eyes, though, I suspect you got those from your father. Whomever he may be."

My head is spinning. Faster than I can keep up with.

Too much.

Every single bit of this night is just too much.

Monsters. These people are monsters.

Ripping off heads. With glowing red eyes.

I've been abducted by monsters.

"She's spiraling," the woman says, who has been so very quiet this whole time that I forget she's even here. "We need to do something about it."

"Hmm," Edmond says, looking at me.

My vision is getting dark. I'm breathing too fast.

"I'll do it."

"Fine," he says.

Suddenly, there's a sharp prick in my neck.

And then nothing but black.

CHAPTER 5

"WAKE UP."

The voice pierces through the fog like a laser beam straight to my eye.

"You should wake up."

Even though my brain has snapped to consciousness, it still takes a monumental amount of effort to drag my eyelids open.

Everything is a dull yellow blur. Fuzzy shapes that move around. And a searing pain in my neck. Blinking rapidly, my vision slowly comes into focus. Pain stabs through my neck as I straighten it, raising my head.

Through the darkness last night, I couldn't see that there are four long windows high up on the back wall. But now dull morning light creeps in through them.

Morning.

I've been here, tied to this chair, all night long.

My head whips to the side. Slumped in it, still chained and bound, is Eli. I watch him, and finally see his chest slowly rise and fall.

I look around, and there's the woman, pacing the room. She fidgets, unsure what to do with her hands, so she twirls the stake she confiscated from Eli. There's no sign of Edmond.

"They'll be back any minute," she says, though she doesn't look at me. Her eyes remain trained on that steel door, even as she paces back and forth. "I thought you might want to be awake and aware when they get here."

"They?" I ask. My voice is scratchy, rough. I realize my tongue is incredibly dry. My throat feels uncomfortable.

"Edmond, and...him," she says. "And anyone else he chooses to travel with."

Tiredness sweeps through me and my eyelids sag closed. My body feels sluggish and heavy.

What did they drug me with?

"They're almost here," she says, and I hear something in her voice that sets me on alert, waking me up: fear. She shuffles, unsure of where to stand. She goes behind me, then seems to think better of it and goes to stand just before the door. "Wake up. You want to be fully aware for this."

"What..." I begin to question. But I hear tires on gravel. And then the sound of three car doors closing.

The woman takes a quick intake of breath and I can feel the terror rolling off of her.

A cold, wet vice creeps up my chest. Up my throat. Around my arms.

Anxiety spills into every vein I have.

The breath catches in my throat.

Because there is suddenly this…presence.

Of darkness.

Of…

The door opens, and that last emotion becomes crystal clear.

Power.

Every cell in my body has stopped replicating. Every hair has stopped growing. Every bit of oxygen has stopped flowing through my body.

I am utterly still. Utterly frozen, as the door slides open, and a figure is revealed.

I hardly even dare call him a man, the person who stands there.

Black slacks hug toned legs. Cinch around a trim waist. A perfectly tailored suit jacket stretches over obviously strong shoulders and lean forearms. A black shirt is buttoned up to the neck, and he wears a blood red tie.

A perfectly sculpted jaw is covered by a short dusting of dark facial hair. He boasts a slightly too-full upper lip. A proud, straight nose. Incredibly thick, nearly black hair is styled modern and to precision.

But it's his eyes that pierce me down to my core.

Dark eyes, that I realize are a dark, forest green, pin me.

He swears. He says it in something I think might be German, but somehow I know that he swears.

"Hello, Logan Pierce."

His voice sends an echo reverberating throughout my entire body.

It snatches me around the chest and draws me close.

My entire body trembles. And I can't even breathe, much less say a word.

"You did well in calling me, Edmond of the House of Valdez." The man steps inside, slowly, one controlled step at a time, across the concrete floor. "She does look just like her."

Who? I mentally say. *Who is it you think that I am?*

The man's eyes flick over to Eli and a little smile curls on his lips. "Oh, that clever little whore. Thinking she can send her father's man-servant to hide and protect her child for all these years." He looks over to Edmond, who steps into the space. "How much longer until Rath awakens?"

Edmond looks down at his watch. "Any moment now, your Majesty."

Majesty?

My head is spinning again. My heart seems to have taken up residence outside of my body. Like it sits in this man's hand, as he slowly, so very slowly, paces around the room, looking me over.

Finally, he comes to a stop, standing directly in front of me. His dark eyes bore into me with such intensity that I'm pretty sure I'm just a bare, bone white skeleton now, shackled to this chair.

"Is it true that you have no idea who Alivia Ryan Conrath is?" he asks.

His lips. Oh, lord, why can't I look away from his lips as he speaks?

"No," the word squeaks from my lungs as I finally look up to his eyes. "Though I've heard that word—name—Conrath, said several times since I was...brought here."

The man continues to study me and my breath catches again.

Power. Dominance. Fear. It radiates off of him in waves.

"I was told you were adopted," he says. "How old are you, my love?"

A shiver crackles its way down my core at his last two words. I try to speak; only the words catch in my throat. This is bullshit. All of it. Last night. This space. These people. I lick my lips, holding his eyes warily. "I just turned twenty a few weeks ago."

His only reaction to that is that his eyes narrow slightly. I can practically see the gears turning in his head.

Whatever this is, he's piecing it together as well.

But my eyes fall downward. And I see his fingers curl into fists.

"Release her," he commands, and that's exactly what it is. A command.

Edmond scrambles forward. With a key, he releases me from the chains. I rub my wrists and stretch through the soreness in my entire body from sitting in one position all night. I remain sitting, though.

"What of your birth father?" he asks. His voice is low. Intimate. Words meant for only the two of us.

I shake my head. "Nothing. My parents never knew

anything at all about either of my birth parents. I was placed with them when I was three days old."

His eyes narrow again, trying to puzzle this, whatever this is, together. "And what of him?" the man says, nodding his head toward Eli. "I assume Rath has been watching over you in some form or another since you were…" He pauses, mentally calculating something. "Four years old?"

I blink three times. "Four? I…I didn't meet Eli until I was fourteen."

The man looks over at Edmond. "You're sure your contact at the House of Conrath said sixteen years?"

Edmond nods. "That's what she said."

"Why do you keep calling him Rath?" I ask, looking from Edmond, to the man staring at me.

"What is it you call him?" he asks, genuine curiosity in his eyes. "Eli?"

I nod. "Cornelius," I say. "Cornelius Rath. Eli for short. Why would you call him by his last name?"

There's a slight sparkle in the man's eye and an amused smile begins curling in the corner of his mouth. "Cornelius. I don't think even Henry knew his real name, if *Eli* is telling you the truth."

Henry. There is another one of those names I know has meaning, but don't understand the history of.

I'm beginning to realize that maybe I don't know very much about my life.

A tiny moan pulls my attention to Eli, who still sits slumped over, his eyes closed.

"Right," the man says. "I suppose we ought to get the

entire purpose of this trip over with before *Cornelius* wakes and makes things much more difficult."

He offers a hand to me. Looking up into his eyes, I see that there is no other option than to take it. I place my hand in his, and there's a vibration that surges through my entire body at the connection. Ice. Fire. Time.

My eyes widen as I look up at his and I stand. His widen just slightly, staring at my hand. And I wonder if he felt it, too.

"It will be over in just a moment," his voice comes out wispy, full of anticipation.

And suddenly, he raises my wrist. Sharp fangs lengthen and sink into my flesh.

Searing pain rips through my body, but the next moment, I find myself falling instantly still. The man's arms wrap around me, holding me upright. And a thick fog sweeps through me, numbing my body, numbing my brain.

I hear him make a little sound. An excited moan. Another, harder, more insistent.

And then he releases me. My brain only begins to register my surroundings when I see him lick over the puncture wounds in my wrist, and they immediately close up.

"She's Royal," the man breathes. I blink, finding myself face to face with this man and his black-green eyes. "Through *both* sides. Mother and father. A descendant of Dorian and Malachi."

My head rolls, my muscles weak and tired. I blink, slow.

Wake up.

Open your eyes.

So I do. I force them open.

And stare into this man's eyes.

"Two Royal bloodlines," he breathes, warming my face. My skin tingles. "There has not been word of a female Royal Born in over ten years. Not since Aster Dawes."

And I see things in his expression now that were not there just moments ago. Reverence. And something that looks inexplicably like hope.

"She still has so much life ahead of her."

My head whips to the side to see Eli's head rising, his dark eyes watching us.

"It doesn't have to happen yet," he says. There's defeat in his eyes. Agony. Failure. "Please give her a little more time."

"Did you know?" the man says accusingly. He still gently cradles me against his chest, supporting me while the strength returns to my legs. "Did you know that both her bloodlines were Royal?"

Eli's eyes just stare darkly at the man. His lips press into a thin line, his jaw clenched tight.

"Do you know who her father is? Her blood is both of Dorian and Malachi. Alivia is a descendant of Dorian, so he must be of Malachi." His tone grows more frantic. More desperate.

"Alivia never told me who the man was," Eli—Rath says. "Only that she knew he was a Royal."

But instead of being angry, this man's breathing only grows harder in excitement. I feel it sparking off of him in waves. A tidal wave that could take both of us under.

"Please," I breathe, finally finding myself again. "I don't

understand. Who are you? Who is it you think I am?"

The man's eyes once more come to mine, and that excitement does not diminish. "Who you may be is why you must die."

Once more, his fangs lengthen. His eyes ignite brilliant, blood red.

"No!" The word rips from Eli as he surges forward, his restraints groaning.

And a scream cuts from my throat. I throw my hands up, shoving back against his chest.

But he does not look deterred. His hold around me does not loosen.

"No, please," I beg. "You don't need to kill me."

"Yes," he breathes. His gaze is misty, excited. "I actually do. And I pray, I pray a thousand and one prayers that you will understand why in a few days' time."

Staring into his brilliant glowing red eyes, I fear. But I'm also ready to *fight*.

"You can't kill me," I say, my voice turning hard and even. "I don't even know your name."

The look in his eyes softens, but there is also something sad in them. "Oh, my love, I pray that soon you will remember that, too."

"Let her go, *Cyrus*," Eli barks, as if he can order this man around.

A hiss blows over his lips and he turns to bare his teeth at Eli.

A terrified storm calms in me.

Cyrus.

Cyrus.

"Cyrus," I say softly. And like a calming wave washes over him, he looks back at me. His eyes widen. His mouth hangs slightly slack. And I don't know what brave, idiotic instinct in me makes me do it, but I raise my hand to rest it against his cheek. "You want to kill me, but you don't even know me. How is that fair?"

He blinks once, slow. "I'm afraid in our world, the word *fair* applies very little."

Our world.

"I say you must die so that you can awake in four days' time and be like myself," he says quietly. "So you may learn the truth of your world, your birthright. The truth of your vampire heritage."

Vampire.

The word echoes through me over and over, banging against the back of my brain. Against the hollow places in my lungs. Down over the bones in my legs.

Vampire.

Not real. *Not real*, my brain wants to scream.

But it's there right in front of me.

A set of gleaming fangs. A pair of glowing red eyes.

"You must die so that we can know who you truly are," Cyrus says.

I blink. His body is pressed against mine, and I suddenly have to ask myself why I haven't been recoiling from this stranger who is telling me that I must die.

"No one tells you no, do they?" I breathe. Because I see that it's true. His eyes, the expressions of everyone else in this room, confirm it. "If there is no other option, I have a demand."

His nostrils flare slightly, his eyes widen just a bit.

"A deal," I say. "You'll kill me. But you have to give me…two months to say goodbye to my family and friends. To finish my life. You don't even know me, and you want to kill me. You owe me at least that."

There's a little spark of excitement in his eyes, and I have to wonder if I've triggered something.

"I can give you a week," he says.

"Logan," Eli hisses. "You don't know what you're doing."

"A week isn't enough," I say, shaking my head and steeling my gaze. "Seven weeks."

"Two," Cyrus counters. And a tiny little smile begins curling on his lips.

"A month," I say loudly, glaring at him. "I'll bargain no further."

And that smile grows full. It reveals perfectly straight, white teeth. A stone does a little skip in my chest.

"Deal," he says. "But in exchange, I will be with you at all times. Lest you decide you stand a chance at running."

I swallow. *At all times.*

"Fine," I say. "But I will up the stakes. During that month, you have to get to know me, really *know* me. And maybe at the end of that month, you'll think twice about me having to die."

His smile broadens. And I can't help the little one that tugs at my own face.

"Oh, my love, I shall take your offer to get to know you." His eyes darken with plotting. "But the final chip to our bargain is that I will take Rath into custody, and he shall not be released until you are dead."

And before I can react, Cyrus clasps his hand around mine, shaking hard, his eyes boring into mine while he smiles that conniving smile of his.

Eli roars, raging against his bonds, snapping another bolt.

"Edmond," he says, releasing me and taking a step away. "The House of Valdez will keep Rath in their custody until mine and Logan's deal comes to a close. He is not to be released until then."

"Yes, your majesty," Edmond says. He and the woman rush forward, and with a speed I can hardly track, they unleash Eli from the chair, binding him and dragging him to his feet. Not another moment of hesitation for further instruction, they begin dragging him toward the door.

"Eli!" I scream. Though I don't know what else to say. Everything is moving at lightning speed, and I don't stand a chance of keeping up.

"Logan!" he bellows, looking over his shoulder back at me. "Cyrus is a snake. You watch every move. And never forget he has two faces!"

But then he's out the door, and Edmond shoves another needle into his neck, just before shoving his collapsing body into the back seat of a vehicle.

"That was nice and clean, wasn't it?" Cyrus says, looking back at me with a little smile. "Let us move on to closing your human life, shall we?"

CHAPTER 6

SLOW DOWN, SLOW DOWN!

My brain is screaming the two words on repeat. Too fast, too much. This is all insane. Too much.

I sit in the back seat of a huge SUV, Cyrus at my side, looking around the town as we roll down the street. He wears a dark pair of sunglasses. As does the driver. A pale white man, who I'm guessing is actually an albino. And the woman sitting in the passenger seat. She's tall but very thin. Her face looks like it was sculpted by razor blades. She may be the most beautiful woman I've ever seen, but she's terrifying.

Cyrus introduced them as Fredrick and Mina.

I didn't even manage words to them.

I guide them to my apartment building, wishing the journey took so much longer, but really, we were only four blocks away.

Fredrick turns the vehicle into the parking lot.

"You say the transaction has already closed?" Cyrus asks, looking at my building with wary disgust.

"Yes, your Majesty," the man says in shaky English. "The realtor will meet us there with the keys."

"Good," he says with a curt nod. He turns to me in the seat. "You have ten minutes to go inside and collect your belongings. Mina will be watching you the entire time, so you may wish to reconsider running."

With a dark look over her shoulder, Mina climbs out of the vehicle and slips off into the parking lot.

"Am I coming back to my apartment?" I ask, my voice quivering.

"Not for a while," Cyrus shakes his head, his eyes rising up to the seedy building. "I don't stay in places like this. We'll be going to live somewhere much more...comfortable."

I swallow. "My friend... She comes over a lot. She'll wonder what's going on. What...what am I supposed to tell her?"

Cyrus smiles, something terrifying. "I pray that you're a quick-thinking liar. You should have thought of this before we made our bargain this morning."

Prick.

My hands roll into fists, but I just clench my jaw tight and open the car door.

This mad man is taking control of my life. Making me move in with him?

I pause for just a moment.

I remember the eviction notice taped to my door

yesterday.

I was two weeks away from being homeless.

Look on the bright side, Logan, I think to myself. At least now you won't be living in your car.

Oh, hell.

Amelia's car is there in the parking lot, just to the side of our stairs. Of course she would be here when I'm coming home with dangerous people lurking over my shoulder.

I take the stairs slowly, stalling, while my brain scrambles to come up with a story. Any kind of explanation as to why I'm about to disappear on her.

My hand falls on the knob, and I unlock it.

The living room is quiet when I walk in. The dining room and kitchen are vacant. Silently, I walk back down the hall, and finally, I hear the sound of water running in the shower.

A brief moment of relief gushes through me. At least I can pack before I have to face her.

In a whirlwind, I throw every bit of clothing I can fit into a duffle bag. My brush. My makeup bag. Everything essential that I will need for at least a week.

Cyrus is going to have to let me come back at some point and deal with my things. Sometime in the next two weeks before the landlord tosses all my stuff out into the parking lot and changes the locks.

"What the hell, Lo?"

I whip around at the angry voice.

Amelia stands there, wrapped in a towel, her hair dripping wet.

"You don't come home last night, you won't answer your

cell, and now I find you sneaking in and packing a bag?" Her face is turning red, seething with anger. "There was a power issue at our place, so we came back here last night around ten. Where were you?"

My mouth opens and closes. I blink once. Twice.

"I'm so sorry," I croon. "I think I lost my cell phone last night. But I kind of…"

Amelia's eyes drop, and she takes in what I'm wearing. They rise up to my disheveled hair. "Oh my… You slept with someone last night, didn't you?"

Her eyes dance with excitement. Suddenly, her mouth drops open. "Was it Eli? Did you finally bang him?"

I know my eyes bug out. My mouth probably pops open, too.

But I force a laugh. And I'm sure I don't have to fake blushing.

"No, not Eli," I say, rolling my eyes and trying to look annoyed—instead of terrified. "But, I did kind of meet someone. And I did kind of stay over last night."

It's not entirely a lie.

Just not entirely the full truth of last night and this morning's insanity.

"Oh, my gosh," she says, shuffling forward, tucking her towel so it doesn't fall. She takes my hands in hers. "Tell me. His name. Is he hot? Is he good in bed? Are you going away for a romantic, spontaneous week?"

I make myself smile, and tell myself that I have to sell this. I have to make her believe it.

"His name is Collin," I lie, and I hardly even hesitate in replacing Cyrus with Collin. "He's…dangerous looking." Not a lie, whatsoever. But I wiggle my eyebrows to sell it to my best friend. "And I dare say he has some experience up his sleeve."

She squeals, throwing her arms around me. "This is amazing, Lo. I mean, I really thought that eventually you and Eli would hook up. But this is even better! When can I meet this new, dangerous Collin?"

My stomach plummets.

Never.

Never, ever, *ever*.

"I don't know," I say, turning and finishing packing my things. "Maybe when we get back. We're going to his cabin in Fairhope for a few days. I already got work off. I guess it depends how this goes."

"This must be pretty serious if you're already going on vacation with a guy you just met last night," she says, coming to sit on the edge of my bed. "Are you sure about this, Lo? I mean, don't get me wrong, I'm super excited about it, but it doesn't really seem like…you?"

I sigh, and zip my bag closed. She's right. Maybe I'm just too harsh and picky, but I rarely find anyone to date that doesn't just annoy me.

I shrug, arching an eyebrow as I turn to face her again. "Who knows, maybe this is the beginning of a new life."

She smiles, and follows me as I haul my bag out.

I stop at the front door. "You and Tanner should go ahead and get engaged. Soon."

"Why?" she asks, her brows furrowing in my sudden change of direction.

I smile, though I'm sure it doesn't look genuine. "Because you love each other. And…life is short."

Amelia gives me a little confused look, but just shakes her head. She gives me another hug, and opens the door for me.

"Oh my…" she says, staring out. The SUV is parked right at the bottom of the stairs. "Is that him?"

Sure enough, from up here, we can see the bottom half of Cyrus' face.

"Yeah," I say around the claws around my throat.

"Um, you failed to mention that he is hot as sin," she goads. "And apparently loaded if he has his own driver."

I think I make a little noise, hopefully in the affirmative.

Amelia gives a wistful sigh. "You have fun. And be careful. Call me when you figure the phone situation out."

"'K," I say, looking back at her as I step out onto the landing.

It won't be the last time I see her. I'll make sure of that. But it feels like a goodbye, all the same.

"Logan," a voice calls from inside the car, sending a finger shiver down my spine.

I turn and walk down the stairs. Fredrick hops out, opening the back and taking my bag. He opens the door for me, and I climb in beside Cyrus once more.

"I don't think I've ever heard the expression 'hot as sin,'" Cyrus says as Fredrick climbs back in and puts the car into gear. "It sounds like a negative description, but the way she said it…"

It takes me a moment to grasp why I feel so…scared, shocked, right now. My eyes go back to the door I walked out of, and then to this car.

"You…" I stutter. "You could hear her from that far away?"

Cyrus looks over at me, and I can tell he's forcing himself to be patient. "Yes," he responds coolly.

I feel my face grow hot now. I look out the window so I don't have to look him in the eyes. "She didn't…she wasn't saying anything bad. But don't go letting it inflate your ego."

Somehow I can feel it when he smiles.

I don't want to think about if what my roommate said about my captor is true or not.

I remember after a moment that we did not collect Mina. When I look around, Cyrus answers my unspoken question.

"She's following behind us in your vehicle," he explains.

I turn around, and sure enough, she follows just behind us in my car.

"But I never gave her the keys," I say, my brows furrowing.

"Mina possesses a multitude of skills that led to me inviting her into my inner circle," Cyrus says evenly.

Apparently she is as deadly as she looks.

We drive across town. To the border between Greendale and Cherico, to where the nicer homes are. We continue toward the outskirts, to where the city gives way to the country.

Fredrick pulls off the main road, to what I realize is a wide driveway. A huge stone fence surrounds the property and an iron gate swings open when we drive up to it.

A beautifully manicured lawn sprawls out before us. Bushes, trees, endless flowers are placed in carefully planned-out beds.

And at the end of the driveway is one of the most beautiful homes I've ever seen. It looks like something out of a TV show.

A great spire tower makes up the front of the home. White stone sides the entire thing and black, heavy-duty windows are sprawled around. To one side, I see four heavy wooden-looking garage doors.

It's so beautiful. Elegant. Elaborate.

"Is this yours?" I ask breathlessly.

"It is now," Cyrus says as Fredrick parks the car next to another. A small, round woman climbs out, looking toward us in wary anticipation.

Fredrick climbs out. Speaks a few words with the woman, taking the keys. She climbs back in her car and drives away.

"You just bought this?" I question. "You've been in Greendale less than, what? Three hours? And you now own a home here?"

He gives me a charmed little smile, one that makes me feel ignorant and foolish. He doesn't say a word as he climbs out the door Fredrick opens and steps out. To my surprise, he quickly walks around the car and opens my door.

He looks at me and holds his hand out for mine.

He has two faces, Eli—Rath had warned before he was drugged and taken away.

I have to remember that, I tell myself. I see it now, and I can just feel it—how charming Cyrus can be when he wants to be. And then how deadly he can turn within one second.

But I take his hand, and let him help me out of the vehicle.

Fredrick and Mina retrieve my bag, as well as a few other suitcases. More than a few. There are eight of them in total besides my own, and I wonder just how long this deadly group planned to stay here after Edmond called them.

We walk up the grand stairs to the door, a massive, twelve foot tall double one. Inserting the keys, Fredrick unlocks it and stands aside for Cyrus to enter first.

The floors are some kind of stone. Marble, perhaps. A double set of ornate stairs curls around the entry and leads up to the upper floor. Walking straight forward, following after Cyrus, there are huge windows overlooking the back yard.

There's a massive swimming pool with a diving board and a slide. A huge patio surrounds it, with a fire pit with built-in seating and a hot tub. Immaculate landscaping surrounds the huge yard.

But here, in the house, I find a big living room off to the right, already furnished with expensive looking leather couches. A big fireplace. And to the left, there's a dining table with chairs for ten. And a spectacular kitchen.

"Do you approve?" Fredrick asks, looking around, his expression slightly nervous.

"Yes," Cyrus says, casting little more than a glance

around at his surroundings. "This will do fine for the next month."

The next month. That is all Cyrus plans to spend in this grand, beautiful house.

I'm beginning to think *loaded* doesn't cover the financial status of Cyrus.

"Shall we explore the upper floor?" Cyrus says, looking over at me and cocking an eyebrow.

I can't find my voice, but I manage an affirmative squeak.

As a group, the four of us climb the stairs. At the top, we find a hallway that splits. There are three bedrooms off to the left, and two to the right.

Every one of them has their own adjacent bathroom and massive closet. But the obvious master suite houses a massive king-sized bed with a beautiful four-poster frame. Big windows look down over the back yard. And the adjoining bathroom has a spa tub that could fit four people inside. And the shower could fit an entire orgy.

"Considering my companions and myself require little to no sleep, I suggest you enjoy this beautiful space," Cyrus says as we walk around the picturesque master suite. Not another word required, Fredrick immediately takes my bag to the closet and begins unpacking my things.

"You don't sleep?" The words doubtfully slip out before I can actually think them over. Warily, I look over, meeting Cyrus' eyes.

He's staring at me, searching for something. But I don't know what.

"Vampires require very little of it. I sleep perhaps a few

hours a week," he answers me. "Our kind possesses a certain level of…awareness. It makes it very difficult to shut down. And our bodies don't need it the same as humans."

I nod, as if I can comprehend any of that.

"You're handling all of this quite calmly," Cyrus says. "I'm actually somewhat concerned. You don't think all of this is real yet, do you?"

And just like that, as if he's slapped me across the face with the bible of truth, I take one step back. He's nailed it.

"How can I?" I say, shaking my head. A breathy scoff of a laugh shoots over my lips. "Everything has just been…too much. Too many crazy elements. One, that you've kidnapped me. Two, you've taken my friend as hostage. Three, that you say I have to die and have a specific date set for it. And four, that now there is this whole big world that's somehow existed in secret. Vampires." I huff another little laugh. "Forgive me if I can't come to terms with any of it as reality, when just yesterday I was laughing with my best friend about boys."

Cyrus continues to stare at me, watching. He is quiet for a long moment.

Those eyes. Even though his stare is penetrating and somewhat terrifying—Cyrus has the most intense eyes of anyone I've ever seen—I can't get enough of them. I'm pretty sure I could sit and look into them for hours.

"Forgive me, Logan Pierce," he finally says. "In my haste for answers, I sometimes forget that some of the Royals are people with actual lives before they get thrown into this world. You should rest." He turns, heading for the door, leaving me standing by the bed. Fredrick immediately takes the hint and exits the room. "Come and find me when you're ready for some answers."

He glances at me once more, an open expression there that I can't quite identify. And then he closes the door behind him. Leaving me alone.

CHAPTER 7

I STAND THERE IN THE ROOM FOR A LONG TIME, STARING AT the door. Listening to Cyrus' footsteps walking away. Hearing him quietly speak with the others.

He's left me on my own. But I don't think for one second that all three of them aren't acutely aware of every one of my movements.

I'm a prisoner. What am I supposed to do with myself?

Still aching from being shackled to a chair all night, and smelling like an auto body shop, I head into the bathroom.

It takes nearly twenty minutes to fill up that giant tub. But finally, it rises to the top, and I climb inside. A sigh escapes my lips as I slide into the hot water, the jets gently blowing massaging strokes over my body.

Don't think. You don't have to think right at this moment, I tell myself.

So I close my eyes and just focus on the black of the back of my eyelids.

~

THE WATER IS LUKEWARM WHEN MY HEAD NODS AND I JERK awake, splashing water all over the floor. I look around, taken over by confusion for a moment. Trying to figure out where the hell I am.

And it all comes crashing back.

Right.

Pulling the drain, I slip out, grabbing a towel hanging on the hook. I marvel at how the entire house was furnished with absolutely everything, just ready for Cyrus and his crew— and me—to walk right in and set up life.

I can only imagine how much it must have cost him.

Going to the closet that Fredrick has already organized, I pull out a pair of shorts and a tank top. Twisting my hair up into a knot at the top of my head, I decide this is as good as it needs to be for now.

I'm not trying to impress anyone.

I stand in front of the bedroom door for a full two minutes. Which is bullshit. Absolute bull.

This is my life. Cyrus, the crazy psycho just stormed into it, making demands, flashing his fangs. Telling me he won't release Eli until I'm dead.

Okay. I may be his prisoner here. That doesn't mean I have to be pleasant company in the meantime. That doesn't mean I can't take full advantage of my time living in this beautiful house when I was just about to become homeless.

Give him hell.

Yanking the door open, I step out into the hall.

The upstairs sounds quiet as I walk down the hall. My ears strain for sounds, and I hear something downstairs.

The house has transformed since I went into my room. Now, as I walk down the grand stairs, I see that heavy wood shutters have been pulled closed over the windows. They block out nearly all of the late afternoon light outside. The house is nearly dark.

"Hello?" I call, rounding the entryway, being careful to navigate through the dark house.

The sound of a knife cutting stops. "We're in here." Fredrick's choppy English cuts through the dark.

I step into the living area and find Fredrick in the kitchen, working at a rapid pace. The room smells divine. Something with garlic and maybe cilantro. And the smell of flour and eggs.

"I hope you were able to get some rest."

Cyrus' voice pulls my eyes to the right. I see him and Mina sitting on the couches, tablets in their hands, numbers and information sprawled across the screens.

"As good as can be expected when you're a prisoner to a crazy man who says he's a vampire," I say. I walk right in and flop down on the couch opposite of where he sits.

Mina mutters something to Cyrus in German and then leaves, Fredrick following after her without a word. Leaving me alone with Cyrus.

I watch them leave. I can't decide if I feel better or worse with them gone.

"Is that where you're from?" I ask, folding my legs up under me. "Germany?"

Those dark eyes bore into me. My eyes slowly adjust, dilating so that I can see better in the dim light that creeps in around the shutters. Cyrus' lips are pressed together in a thin line. He sits with his legs crossed, one arm stretched out across the back of the couch.

He's been in this house for all of a few hours, yet he seems perfectly at home.

Cyrus seems rather adaptable.

"Austria has been my home for a very long time," he says. "Though you could say I am rather well traveled. I've seen all of the world. Though I will say I've been to the States more than I'd prefer in the last little while."

My throat tightens at that, cracking the hard façade I'm building. I don't want to think about it, because for my entire life, I've trained myself not to wonder, not to worry about it.

But it's the first place my brain goes.

"Was one of those times because of...her?" I ask. "The one you say I look like?"

Cyrus continues studying me. "There's no doubt about it, Logan. Alivia Ryan Conrath *is* your birth mother. I tasted it in your blood. The resemblance is spectacularly obvious. But to answer your question, yes, one of those times was because of her. The last, because of your cousin's mother."

My traitorous stomach does a little somersault. "I have a cousin?"

"Oh yes," Cyrus says with a little smile. "She'll one day be the leader of the House in the northeast part of this country. Though that's still some years away. The girl is only ten years old, currently. And if I recall, she also has a younger brother. Though he isn't a Royal."

I shake my head.

All these words. He keeps saying all these crazy words.

"I apologize," Cyrus says. Briefly, he looks away, studying the beautiful home that is now his. But he looks back at me, pinning me with those eyes. "I speak as if you are familiar with our world. You look so much like Alivia, that I forget that she kept you removed from this world."

"Do you know her well?" I blurt. I actually bite down on my stupid tongue.

I don't want to wonder.

I don't want to ask questions.

I love my family. Even if we don't share blood, I wouldn't trade them for anything or anyone.

But I keep asking.

Something in Cyrus' expression darkens. One corner of his upper lip twitches. "Oh, I spent a good deal of time with her."

"What is she like?" I whisper.

Again, I wonder at the hardness that takes over Cyrus' face when I mention this woman he says is my biological mother. She can't be a good person, if someone like *him* has this kind of reaction to even the mention of her name.

"She's smart, brave," Cyrus says. "Also cunning and manipulative. Which makes her very fit for our world. But considering the history between she and I, we both try to avoid one another as much as possible."

It makes my chest tighten. Cunning. Manipulative. Not positive words.

It makes me look at myself. Would I use those words to describe myself? Did I inherit any of that from her?

"It sounds like maybe you were in love with her," I say, looking back up at Cyrus.

A little hiss rumbles in his chest and red embers ignite in his eyes. "Your mother led me to believe she was someone she is not, all to try to repair the broken heart her now husband gave her. Alivia knows how to use people to get what she wants and needs."

I squeeze my eyes closed and shake my head. I hate this. I want to take back the last few questions and get rid of the information I've just learned.

Then I could always hope that my biological mother was out there, being a good person. Someone who influenced the world for the better.

Instead, I'm being told about someone who sounds terrible.

"Do you know where she lives?" I ask. Because I can't stop.

Cyrus doesn't answer right away. My eyes slide back open, and I find mine fixed on his.

"Are you sure you want the answers to these questions?" Cyrus asks. "Your family's legacy is a dark and complicated one."

I swallow once. "That will be the last one I ask about her," I say. "For now."

Cyrus sighs, but nods. "I suppose it is understandable to wish to know about your bloodline. Perhaps one day we will solve the mystery of who your father is." He pauses, as if mentally running through who the possibilities are. As if he would know. "Your mother lives in Mississippi, where she is leader of the House of Conrath."

I shift, drawing one knee up to my chest. "You keep saying that word—House. What does that mean?"

There is a big moment of both of us holding our breath.

This is the meat.

The bigness that's coming to sweep over me.

I might not yet accept that this is real. But once Cyrus shares this information, I don't think there's any going back.

"There are a lot more of us than you might think," Cyrus says. "We've been around for thousands of years. There are generations and generations, families. Wars. With thousands of us around, there has to be some kind of governance. There has to be a system in place to keep our kind a secret."

He slowly rubs his hands together. There's weight in the way he speaks. History. As real and tangible as Paul Revere, or Harriet Tubman, or Nero. This is Cyrus' reality.

"There are twenty-seven Houses throughout the world, spread out by population," he continues. "There are three kinds of vampires in the world. The Bitten, who are created, by accident usually, when a vampire drinks too much of a human's blood but does not kill them. The creation of a

Bitten has been illegal for several years now, and there hasn't been one reported in…seven or so years."

That, in itself right there, sounds like a huge story. A big piece of history that he summed up in just a few sentences.

"And then there are the Born. Common citizens, you might call them." Cyrus' fingers roll, forming a fist on his left hand, his knuckles turning white. "And there are the Royal Born. The ones with Royal linage. These are those who are given charge of ruling the world from the shadows. Of keeping our kind—in all their forms—in check."

I realize I'm leaning forward, listening, on bated breath.

"Here in the United States there are three Houses," he explains. "Your mother, Alivia, rules the House of Conrath, based in Mississippi. She governs all of the South. Edmond Valdez, who you met last night, is the second son of the ruler of the House of Valdez, based in Las Vegas. The situation in the north east, where your cousin will one day rule, is a bit more complicated until she comes of age."

"My cousin," I say. "How is she tied?"

"Your mother, while still human, fell in love with a man who did not realize he was, in fact, a Born." At my confused expression, he waves a hand. "We'll get to all of that shortly. But this man, Ian Ward," again, tightness sounds in his voice. It seems Cyrus' experiences with everyone in that region are not positive. "Has a younger sister, Elle."

But at *her* name, his tone softens. "She wanted to escape the never ending drama Alivia brings with her, so she moved to Boston. There was bad blood between your mother and the ruling family there—the Allaways. Charles Allaway wanted to punish Ian. So he took Elle, and artificially inseminated her. It took. She became pregnant with a Royal heir. She killed Charles Allaway before the child was born. So now, Elle and her husband—I don't recall his name—are raising her to be the kind of leader they wish her to be."

So much. So big and so complicated. This world. This family Cyrus claims I am a part of.

"Back to the Houses," Cyrus changes direction. "There is also a House in Vancouver, which rules over the North West region of the States, as well as western Canada. Every section of the world is divided out, and responsibility given to a family or group of Royal Born."

"Which is what you say I am," I clarify. "You say I am one of you, but I don't have fangs. I've never had the strength to rip anyone's head clean from their shoulders."

"Because you have not died your first death yet."

The words settle heavy.

"A Born, common or Royal, is conceived by a human mother and a Born father. But eventually, when that human dies, their vampire DNA is sparked to life. You will lie there, dead for all the world to believe, but in four days' time, you will Resurrect, as your true self. A Born."

"Resurrect," I whisper the word.

Cyrus nods. "We get to experience two deaths. One as a human. And eventually, always under bloody circumstances, as a vampire."

"Is that supposed to mean vampires are immortal, if it takes violence?"

Cyrus' lips form a thin line. He nods his head, his

eyes dark.

Looking at Cyrus, I search for signs. To my eyes, he appears to only be in his upper twenties. But the way he speaks, the power he wears like a crown, I have to wonder.

"How old are you?"

His expression does not change or give anything away. "Old."

We stare one another down. Neither giving in. Neither confessing that any of the words spoken in the last twenty minutes are a joke.

But still, I huff a laugh. I shake my head.

"So this is why you say I have to die," I state, letting my eyes wander the room, not really seeing anything. "Because you will kill me. But after I'm dead, after four days, I'll wake back up. As a vampire?"

I look back at Cyrus. Still stone serious. He gives a little nod. "Correct."

Half a breath, I hold it. "And then what?" I ask. "What will be the rules of my new life? What can I expect?"

All this time, Cyrus has not moved a muscle. He still sits with his arm over the back of the couch. The picture of controlled, dangerous perfection.

"You'll crave blood," he says. "It was a curse, that we crave the blood of our former kind. It will be…" he draws out. "Difficult to control, for a time. But you'll also feel incredible. Like your best day of health, times one hundred. You'll be strong, capable. Never to be ill again. You'll be fast, nearly indestructible. So long as you avoid stakes and blades."

I swallow.

Guess some of the stories are true.

Eli was carrying a stake. And how could he know we would run into vampires at the time?

"And the sun will not be your friend," Cyrus continues. "Your eyes will not be able to handle the direct sun. You will prefer the night. It will feel natural, the change to a nocturnal schedule."

"And what about my life?" I ask. "When I'm craving the blood of every single person I know? What about my job? My family? If I'm going to want to hurt them, what then?"

Finally, Cyrus moves. He shifts, both of his feet on the floor. He leans forward, his elbows on his knees. His dark eyes bore into mine, and I now realize just how much my eyes have adjusted. I see his clearly. They dilate big and wide, taking all of me in.

"That is what these four weeks are for," he breathes. I hear it in his tone, how difficult giving me those four weeks is. And I still don't understand why this has to happen *now*. "For once your human life is over, you will be stepping into a whole new world. A new birthright. And you have no idea the wonders and horrors that await you."

Without another explanation, he rises and walks to the kitchen, picking over the food Fredrick has been preparing.

And I sit on the couch, feeling utterly lost. Completely overwhelmed.

But something stirs inside of me. Something excited. Something antsy. Something a little deadly.

CHAPTER 8

THE STONE WALLS ARE GLITTERING.

Like crushed diamonds were mixed into the pressed earth, they sparkle and shine.

I turn, taking in the dim red light that refracts off their surfaces. And as I turn, the space opens up. Wide, so high. Great beams span the air above me. A glittering black chandelier hangs overhead. And from somewhere in the room, beautiful music floats through the space.

Faces. But not faces. All around me. Masks, exposing glowing red eyes.

And I'm surrounded by sweeping, swishing fabric.

Men and women float around the room, dressed in opulent finery. Gowns. Suits. Feathers and pearls are splashed here and there.

I step forward, the gown around me swishing softly.

Heels click beneath my feet. Soft fabric hugs my face. The tickle of a feather brushes my cheek.

My eyes sweep between dancing couples.

Something in my chest aches.

I take another step forward.

From one corner of the room to the other, my eyes search.

Glowing red. Glistening white.

But instead of fear, I only feel that sense of searching.

Something is missing.

The dancers sweep into a new movement, and a division in the room forms, leaving me standing alone in the center of the room. And there, at the other end of the room, stands a man in an entirely black suit.

A golden mask is affixed to his face. A crown sits atop his head. He stands there, his hands folded in front of him. Those forest night green eyes bore into my soul.

And in my chest there is finally peace.

A puzzle snaps together, all the pieces finally reassembled.

He takes a step toward me, and I feel all the eyes in the room slide to watch.

He takes another. And another.

My body warms as he approaches. And when he stops just a foot in front of me, my heart stops. Decides it no longer needs to keep beating.

I stare into his eyes.

Slowly, he raises his hands, and he takes my mask, and one tiny movement at a time, he lifts it from my face.

My lips fall open slightly, every bit of me waiting. Poised.

"Finally," he breathes. "After all this time."

MY EYES FLY OPEN.

Where just moments ago, my heart stopped, it now races.

My hand slides up to my chest, and it feels hollow.

I look around, confused and disoriented. The massive four-poster bed. The expensive curtains pulled over the window. The open doorway leading to an unfamiliar bathroom.

And I remember.

Three weeks and six days.

It's how long I have to live.

It's how long Eli will remain in custody.

I reach for my cell phone and check the time. 8:41.

My heart ticks into my throat. I scramble from the bed and race for the closet. I throw on the first clothes I can find that will be appropriate for work. I remind myself that I'm not going to be cowed into fear while I'm stuck here. I throw the door to my room open and dash down the stairs.

A voice, harsh and angry, echoes through the house. I round the stairs and dash into the kitchen. In the living room, I see Cyrus, phone pressed to his ear. He's angry. Livid.

Mina sits at the island, a tablet in her hand. She looks up at me as I go to the refrigerator and search for anything to eat.

"You have work today, yes?" she asks in a thick accent.

"Yes," I answer her, realizing it's the first time she's spoken to me. "And if I don't leave right now I'm going to be late."

I settle on a yogurt and grab a banana I see sitting on the counter.

I'm not going to wait for permission to head to work. Our deal was that I could wrap up my life.

He gives an inch, I'm going to take a mile.

I head for the door without looking back.

"Mina will accompany you to your place of employment," Cyrus suddenly says from behind. I pause with my hand on the door, looking over my shoulder. Cyrus stands there, and to my immense pleasure, he seems surprised at my boldness. He holds the phone, tipped away from him for a moment. "I shall meet you there after you're finished."

I curl a nasty smile onto my lips. "Can't wait." I spin on my heel and walk to the front door.

The deadly woman follows me outside. She slips on a pair of dark sunglasses just before we walk out the door. Silent, she slips into the passenger seat of my car.

"I don't know how I'm supposed to explain you to my boss," I say in annoyance as I put the car into reverse and back out. I start down the driveway. "I don't exactly qualify to have a shadow at my work. I'm the apprentice."

"He'll never know I am around," she says, looking all around. She studies the drive in front of us, the side lawn. And I get the feeling she's more than adequate at security. "I do not need to stay directly at your side to keep an eye on you."

I glance over at her before I turn onto the main road. "I still don't really understand. Yes, Cyrus says I'll resurrect after I die. But I don't understand why he, in particular, cares, or why he's in such a hurry."

"That is an answer that is for him alone to provide," she responds simply, and her silence tells me she's done with this conversation.

So with only the quiet drone of the radio, we make our way through town. I round the block to my work, and park at the side of the building. With a wary look in Mina's direction, I climb out.

I walk to the front doors, and look over my shoulder. Just as I pull it open, I see Mina blow a kiss to me and slink into the shadows of the building.

How? How did my life get so weird in less than two days?

Things are quiet when I get inside. I head to Emmanuel's office and find him at his desk.

"Morning," he says distractedly as he stares at his screen. "How was your weekend?"

I actually chuckle. How am I supposed to answer that question?

"It had lots of unexpected turns of events," I say. And realize that was dumb. If he asks questions...

But he only makes a grunt noise, his eyes still fixed on the screen.

"I assume today's a down day?" I ask, placing a hand on the doorframe. "Down to the dungeon for me?"

He takes a few seconds too long to respond, and when he makes some kind of affirmative noise again, he looks over at me, blinking four times, as if he's just realized I'm standing here. "Sorry, Logan. Some administration stuff going on this morning." His eyes flick to the screen again. "Yes, take today and let's get everything all cleaned up. Thanks."

I actually smile, shaking my head as I turn and walk out of his office.

I walk out and head down the stairs. Down to the lower level, and down to where I am most comfortable at work.

On slow days like this, when there are no loved ones who have passed beyond the veil, we play catch up. Emmanuel goes about the business of running Sykes Funeral Home. Craig and Katie occasionally come in to help me, but usually they get the day off. But me? I get to clean the prep room.

Meticulously, I clean the tools. I clean out the fridge. I sweep. I dust.

And as I work, I blast my music.

I love alternative. Rock. Punk. Anything loud and passionate and...aggressive. Anything that gets my blood running and gives me the feeling that I can do anything.

Emmanuel calls it awful noise. He says that you can't even understand the words, and constantly questions how I'm not a vile, stupid-people murdering person.

But we like what we like.

True to her word, I never once see any signs of Mina. It's

just me in this building, and considering I never hear Em question anyone who doesn't belong, she stays outside.

I'm grateful for a day like today, where Em and I don't have to work side-by-side, face-to-face. It would be hard to act normal, when everything is turned upside down in my life.

It'd be hard to hide the constant worry twisting in my gut.

Cyrus ordered that Eli be taken into custody. Somewhere, Eli is tied up, watched over by Edmond Valdez. Possibly taken back to Las Vegas, where Cyrus says they live.

Is he okay? Will they hurt him?

I still as I wipe down the table.

I've known Eli since I was a freshman in high school. Spent countless hours with him. Accepted him as a part of my life.

But Cyrus says it's been sixteen years since he disappeared from Mississippi. What if... Is there any chance that he's really been there, quiet, in the shadows, for nearly my entire life?

Who is Eli? Because apparently, he is not the man that I came to think of as a family member.

At three-thirty I've cleaned every surface of the prep room. I've organized the casket selection room twice. The chapel is as clean as ever. So I pack up my things and walk upstairs.

Like he hasn't moved a muscle, Emmanuel still stares at that computer screen.

"Need anything else?" I ask. He's working so intently, I'm actually a little concerned. He's not usually so absorbed.

"Thank you, Logan," he says. "I'll see you tomorrow."

A sad little smile on my lips, I turn, and head outside.

I'm only two steps down the stairs when Mina steps out of the shadows, sunglasses still in place.

"Did you enjoy your boring day of waiting for me to run?" I ask as I head to my car. Sweat immediately breaks out onto my forehead. It's hot, summer ramping up to full swing.

"Delightful," she mutters. We both slide into the seats and I start the engine, cranking the air conditioning.

"I thought Cyrus was going to meet us after I got off," I say.

But at the same moment the words are out of my mouth, a sleek, black car pulls up beside mine. The back window rolls down, and Cyrus looks over at us through his black shades.

I roll my window down, a sense of dread and excited anticipation creeping up my throat.

"I hope you had a pleasant day," he says. And the vibrations of his voice send goose bumps flashing over my arms.

I don't know what to say. No, it wasn't a pleasant day. Really, in any aspect.

"Follow me," he says. And his window rolls back up, and he disappears behind the dark tint of his windows.

I let out a big breath. I didn't realize I had been holding it in.

The black car pulls out onto the main road and I follow it as it turns right. I pull in a breath, about to ask Mina where we are going, but I remember that she doesn't want to talk to me, and she is not my friend, even though she's sitting in the seat that is usually only occupied by Amelia.

Through town we drive, and we cross the border into Cherico. With a right turn, I see a sign for the Cherico Municipal Airport.

My brows furrow in confusion as I follow behind the black car, and then we park in two of the five spaces in front of a gray hangar.

I'm about to climb out, when my door suddenly opens, and I look up to see Cyrus holding it open. He looks down at me with those shades, and holds a hand out for mine.

Hesitantly, I take it, and he pulls me up and to my feet.

"Follow me, Miss Pierce," Cyrus says, offering a little smile and turning. Briskly, he walks to a small door in the side of the hanger.

I look him over as we walk, and I trail behind him.

Where as Cyrus wore an expensive and powerful suit yesterday, today he wears a pair of jeans that hug his legs and a black button-up shirt.

I didn't fail to notice how he left the top three unbuttoned. Exposing a lean and firm chest.

He holds the door open for me, and I try to ignore the terrified electricity that crackles down my veins as I step inside.

I expected dark, an enclosed space. Instead, I'm blinded.

A huge door, like a garage, is open, so the entire front side of the hangar is open. A big cement floor stretches out. Off to one side is an enclosed office. Out here there are four old recliners, broken down and worn looking. Pictures adorn the walls. All taken from the air.

And just outside the hangar, out in the brilliant light, is a shiny, jet-black helicopter.

"You must be Cyrus."

A man steps out from the office. He sports a thick, but well-manicured gray beard. He wears a black leather jacket, despite the heat, and worn out but well-fitted jeans. "I'm Vince."

"Pleasure to meet you," Cyrus says, accepting the man's outstretched hand.

"I guess I spoke to your assistant on the phone," he says, stuffing his hands in his pockets, standing there so casually, just chatting. If only he knew. "Sounds like your crew came from far out of town."

Cyrus offers a little, thin-lipped smile. "Far, indeed."

"Well, I'm honored you chose Vince Air for your romantic afternoon," he says, his smile indicating that he's catching on that he's perhaps being a little comfortable and casual for a man like Cyrus. "If you'll follow me, we'll get going."

He turns and Cyrus follows.

"Wait," I scramble. "You said…you said I'd have time. Where are you taking me?"

Cyrus stops abruptly, looking back. And a shiver washes over me. Even though I can't see his eyes, I feel their intensity. Like he is the ultimate predator. And a thrill washes through me, knowing I could never run.

"I keep my promises, Logan," he breathes. He takes three

steps back to me. He reaches out and takes my right hand in his. "I've simply never visited this region. I thought we could enjoy a better view, from the sky. Together."

Shivers.

All over.

Which I hate. But they happen, anyway.

With a little nod, I allow him to pull me forward, and I follow after him.

We climb inside and Vince gets us situated with earpieces and microphones. He shows us how to switch them to a channel so just the two of us can talk without being over-heard by himself. And then we strap in, Cyrus and I, side by side.

I look out, and see Mina and Fredrick watching from the shadowed overhang of the hangar.

"Have you ever ridden in a helicopter before?" Cyrus' voice cuts through my headpiece, his voice sounding mechanical and scratchy.

I shake my head, heavy and cumbersome with the head-piece. "Our family traveled a little bit. My parents liked to vacation. So we've flown a lot. But never in a helicopter."

"You're in for a pleasant experience, then," he says, smiling as the blades above us begin spinning.

And just moments later, we lift into the air.

The pilot gently steers and expertly glides through the air, directing us toward the city.

"You said you've never been to this area," I say, my voice sounding staticky through the headset. "Because this is fairly far from any of the Houses?"

Cyrus glances over at me. He nods.

"My area is ruled by the House in Las Vegas?" I ask. My gut twists. I'm asking questions. Using his words. Using those words of his world. Like I can accept it all. Like I can believe it all is real. "By the...House of Valdez?"

"That's correct," he says. He looks out, his shaded gaze sweeping over the suburbs as we head in the direction of the city.

"And what about you?" I say. "You belong to a House in Austria?"

A little smile curls on his lips but he doesn't look at me. "Not exactly."

Cryptic. Ugh.

"You're someone important," I say, looking down, trying not to think about how much air is between my rear end and that cluster of houses below me. "You aren't being very direct about who you are, but the way Mina and Fredrick look at you? The money? The air around you? You're important."

Again, he doesn't look at me. But I can feel his smile. "Yes," he responds simply.

We glide through the air. The headset crackles and Vince's voice fills my ears. He tells us about the surroundings. He circles the skyscrapers of downtown. Hovers over the Broncos' stadium. Shows us other places of interest in Denver. Places I've visited more than once, but never seen from the air.

And then he banks, and we head toward the mountains.

"Where is the most beautiful place you've ever visited?" Cyrus asks.

I look away, watching as we approach the mountains. "Uh," I think, thinking back through all the trips we took growing up. "I'd say Hawaii, maybe. But there was something…isolated feeling about it. Knowing I was surrounded by all that ocean, and nothing but ocean, for so far, it was a little terrifying, if I'm being honest."

I *feel* Cyrus' eyes narrow on me and wonder what's going through his mind. My eyes dart away from his. "So, I guess it would be the Redwood Forests, in northern California."

Foothills rise below us. And I can't help but think how much more beautiful this tour would be during the winter, when the mountains are capped with snow.

"What about that area captured you?" Cyrus asks. He crosses his ankle over his knee, resting a hand on the opposite one.

I think about his question. And even though I'm looking at the Rocky Mountains, in my mind, I'm back among the moss and gigantic trees.

"I guess it was knowing how old everything there was," I say. "There was this feeling of time there that I don't really know how to explain. That everything there was ancient, but like I was a part of it too. Like we were in a simpler, easier world. The modern world just…didn't matter in those trees. I felt…different there."

I remember the smell. Of water and rotting wood and wild. The air felt different. Thicker. Like it's own alive being that occupied those woods. I remember feeling as if I could disappear in-between those trees and assimilate into a world of mossy knells and sneaking foxes.

"Would you like to visit that feeling again?" Cyrus asks, pulling me from the forest. "Of timelessness?"

My eyes flick to his, and my brows narrow.

Such a strange question.

Such bizarre confidence, like he is powerful enough to obtain even that.

"I wouldn't mind visiting again, if that's what you mean," I say, blinking as I look away, back to the rocky ridges below.

We ride out the rest of the tour in relative silence. Vince guides us through valleys and over high peaks. The mountains stretch up toward us, threatening to scrape the bottom of the mechanical beast. But safely we soar over them.

And finally, we begin making our way back. Over towns. Over homes. Over businesses. Over thousands of lives, and I think about how I only ever get the opportunity to live just one.

Am I doing what I want if I only get to experience this one life?

Hardly.

"Are you alright?" Cyrus asks.

I look over at him. I blink once, taking in his beautiful and terrifying face. The furrowed brows. The lips that hold my gaze. The penetrating eyes.

"Fine," I breathe. "Why?"

"I've only spent hours around you, Logan. But you generally seem to have much to say, and the gall to say it. You've been...pensive."

I look away and shrug. "I'm approaching the end of my life, aren't I?" I say with a little bit of bite and bitterness. "I think this is a perfect time to be pensive."

"Understandable," Cyrus consents.

The night is approaching by the time we land back at the hangar. Deep purples cut through the sky, accompanied by brilliant golds.

I take my headset off and with Vince's hand, climb out. A slight smile pulls on my lips as I look back at the helicopter.

"Thank you for the lovely evening," Cyrus says, shaking Vince's hand once more. "It was a truly beautiful time."

"My pleasure," he says, closing up the helicopter. "You two love birds have a wonderful night."

I startle at his words, looking back.

And as I see Cyrus' little smile once more, as I follow him through the hangar, I can't help but think.

Had this man not come and taken control of my life, had he not kidnapped me, taken away Eli, told me I had to die, would he be the type I'd be interested in?

He's certainly the stuff of a wet dream.

He radiates power.

He's rich.

He has the face of a god.

Certainly plenty of women would kiss his feet and slowly work their way higher.

Had I just run into Cyrus at some random place and he asked me on a date, would I have said yes?

I don't know if I can quite answer that.

Two faces, I remind myself.

"I thought vampires only came out at night," I say, ripping myself in a different direction of thought. "But you're always going out. All of you, always with sunglasses."

"The sun is indeed a problem," Cyrus says, glancing over his shoulder at the sinking sun.

"Sunglasses do the trick, though?" I scoff. "It doesn't seem like it could ever be enough."

Cyrus smiles and stops midway through the parking lot. He pulls the shades off and hands them to me. "These are no ordinary sunglasses. See for yourself."

With a wary look at him, I slip them on.

It's darker. Like the sun was dimmed by half. But there's a feeling…like my eyes don't have to work so hard. Like the light has been uncomfortable all my life, and now they're getting a sudden break.

"They filter out all UV light?" I take a guess.

"It's a lot more complicated than that," Cyrus says, reaching up and removing them from my face. He slips them back on. "But yes, that's the very, very basic explanation of the science put into these."

I realize as we stop in the parking lot that my car is nowhere to be seen. Same with Mina and Fredrick.

"Are you hungry?" Cyrus asks. And surprisingly, he walks to the driver's door and holds it open for…me.

"Uh," I struggle. "I guess."

He smiles and I walk around and slip into the driver's seat. "Then take me to your favorite restaurant." He hands me the keys, and then walks around to get into the passenger seat.

I just look at him for a long moment after he sits and buckles in.

"You don't know how to drive, do you?" I blurt.

That careful, composed façade slips for a moment. A little shade of embarrassment, of humiliation shows itself just for a second.

"There's been little need for me to learn in my very long life," he says, fixing his eyes out the window before us. "Do you think of me as less of a man, now?"

That is when he turns. His eyes bore into mine. As if daring me to say…no.

"It's a basic life skill," I say, swallowing once. I press the ignition button and the engine purrs to life. "You seem the type that could take care of yourself in most situations. Why not this one?"

I look over at him. And he seems…surprised. My answer was not one he expected.

"Would you like to teach me, Logan Pierce?" he asks. And I swear there's a hint of vulnerability there.

Two faces, I think to myself. The vulnerable and sincere. Like this one, right now.

"Alright," I say. I put the car into reverse. "Pay attention as we head to dinner. We'll do the actual driving after."

Words keep spewing out of my mouth as we cut back into Greendale. I rattle off anything and everything I can think of when it comes to driving. Explain the various road signs we see. Point to different parts of the car, explaining what they're for. Even if he probably understands the basics, I talk it all over as if he's never been inside a vehicle before.

By the time we pull into the parking lot of *Carmichaels*, my voice is tired.

But I think I talked some of the pent up energy out of myself.

We walk in, and the waiter seats us at a booth toward the back, in a darker corner.

"You favor Italian food?" Cyrus asks as we both look over the menu.

I shrug. "I like just about everything. But I am always in the mood for their chicken carbonara."

"I know what I'll be ordering, then," he says, setting his menu down and looking over at me as I set down my own.

Which is good timing. The waiter shows up just then and we order.

"So, vampires eat normal food?" I question, keeping my voice low once he's left. Even though no one is seated particularly close to us.

I think Cyrus slipped some money to the waiter.

"Yes," he says, resisting a little smile. "We still require sustenance."

"Not just blood?" I ask, warily.

"No, not just blood," he answers.

He looks up at me, and he settles back into his seat. He looks more relaxed now than earlier. I see a burning desire in his eyes, something inquisitive.

"Your chosen profession is rather unorthodox," he says, jumping right into something heavy. "Tell me. What made you choose it?"

The waiter brings Cyrus a glass of wine, and a glass of water for me.

I pull the glass toward me, running my thumb over the condensation gathering outside it. I look from his eyes to the ice floating in it.

"I'd prefer the real reason," he says, his voice dropping to intimate levels. "Because I suspect there is a very purposeful one."

I look back up at him. And I see that he means it. He wants me to be real and open.

I swallow once. And give it to him.

"When I was eleven, my family was on our way to go camping," I say, letting the pictures float back into my brain. The way the car smelled. How full the back of the minivan was. The frazzled look in my mom's eyes as she tried to remember everything we needed to pack. "My grandparents, my dad's mom and dad, were coming with us."

I take a sip of water. The glass slips through my hand, slick on the outside. But I clasp it harder at the last moment, preventing it from spilling into my lap.

I set it back on the table.

"It started raining just twenty minutes after we left the house," I say. "We were going around this bend at the base of the canyon." The water was coming down so hard. Dad had the wipers going full blast, back and forth, back and forth so fast. "This big truck pulling a trailer came flying down the canyon. He took the turn too wide."

Cyrus leans forward, holding onto every word.

"Dad still blames himself for turning the wheel and

sailing off the road, instead of letting that truck hit us." I swallow. Every once in a while, it hits Dad. He gets real quiet for a day or two. He often just stares at the wall, numb and blank. "We started rolling. Smashing down the hill. Over and over. Glass everywhere. Everyone screaming."

Blood. Snaps. Our things flying everywhere in the car.

"It all happened so, so fast," I breathe. "But I saw it, just for a horrifyingly clear moment. We hit a tree. The branch came crashing through the car. It hit grandpa in the head. And I knew, just was absolutely certain, that he was instantly dead. I knew it, processed all of that, just a second before that branch got me, too."

Whack.

Black.

I realize that Cyrus has reached across the table and is holding onto my wrists while I cling to my cold glass.

"I woke up in the hospital three days later," I continue. My voice sounds rough. Tired. "They said I'd died in the ambulance on the way to the hospital. But they'd pulled me back, and I'd been in a coma for a while after."

I don't remember anything of that time while I lay in that bed. Nothing at all.

"I'll never forget that brief, split second of knowing that my grandpa was dead," I say, looking up at Cyrus. "And since then, I've always wondered where in the world he breathed his next breath."

"You believe in reincarnation?" Cyrus asks quietly.

I just stare at him for a moment, trying to gauge his

reaction. I don't know anyone who has accepted my profound belief. But he shows no sign of scoff. So I nod. "Do you?"

He doesn't answer immediately. I see the thoughts churning behind his eyes. "In a way, absolutely."

I don't really know what that means. But I know I'll never fully understand Cyrus.

"I guess you could say I've been fascinated by death ever since," I say, letting my eyes drop. "After that, I just always had this comfort in being around it. So, being a mortician, it was just the natural course for me."

Cyrus' grip on my wrists tightens just a little. But I don't look. Because I can't stand the intense way he's staring at me.

"Is there anything else I can get for you fine folks?"

The voice cuts between us and I pull away suddenly. The waiter sets our matching dinners down in front of us.

"No, thank you," Cyrus responds, his voice holding a bit of an edge.

WE EAT. CYRUS DOESN'T REALLY SAY MUCH OF ANYTHING else. He's quiet and I can tell he's thinking about something, as if rolling it over and over in his head. Something I said, something from this morning, I'm not entirely sure.

But we finish and he pays. And together, we walk out to the parking lot.

"Are you ready for this?" I ask with a little bit of a smile.

He looks up at me, giving me this challenging look. "Give me the keys."

I toss them to him. Feeling nervous, I climb into the passenger seat. Thankfully it's a Monday, so the parking lot is quiet.

Cyrus starts the ignition. "Foot on the brake," I say. "Put it into reverse, and slowly let off."

He does as I say. And slowly, we back up.

With more than a few jerks and engine revs, we work our way through the parking lot, practicing circling the parking lot of the adjacent hardware store.

He's really not that bad.

My neck is only slightly sore from being jerked a few times.

But after twenty minutes, I think he's ready.

"Let's head back toward the house," I say, nodding my head in that direction. "It's getting dark, the roads are quiet. Think you can handle it?"

He chuckles. A mischievous look comes into his eyes, and he smiles as he points us toward the main road. "Oh, I think I can handle it."

He waits, looking for cars to cross the road.

And as soon as an opening forms, he slams on the gas.

I'm thrown against my seat, a little scream ripping from my lips. But Cyrus guides us between cars, and pulls into our lane of traffic.

He laughs, looking over at me, way too amused.

"Maniac," I chide, righting myself in my seat. I shake my head, even though I smile.

He chuckles, obviously pleased with himself.

I look out at the darkening night, taking in a deep breath. What a strange, strange life I have now.

"You were angry this morning," I say, pulling up conversation. "What were you so upset about?"

Cyrus adjusts his grip on the steering wheel. "There are certain rules in our world. Some are clear, spelled out, written down. Others are unspoken. Some of the Royals in China have been taking advantage of those unspoken rules, and it poses a threat to all our kind."

I consider that for a few moments. "You seem exceptionally involved in the affairs of all the Houses across the globe. What are you, some kind of worldwide ambassador?"

He smiles once more. "Something like that."

"It's really annoying how you do that," I say, looking over at him. "Answering without answering. You like being vague, don't you?"

His dark eyes slide over to mine. "It's easy to become bored after living as long as I have. I find people to be... entertaining when you don't give them exactly what they want."

"So this is all a game to you?" I say, feeling a little hot flare ignite in my chest. "Just messing with me? Keeping me slightly in the dark at all times?"

His eyes dart over to mine. He studies me for another beat too long. Like he's looking for an answer in my eyes. "Yes," he responds. And this time I know he's being honest.

"You know that playing with people makes you an asshole, right?" I bite, raising an eyebrow.

He only laughs, and for some unexplainable reason, I find myself smiling.

We arrive back at his house safely, and with a few too quick stomps on the brake, he parks the car in the garage.

"I hope you had an enjoyable evening, Logan," he says as we walk inside. I see no signs of Mina or Fredrick. "I think I learned some very interesting facts about you today."

My stomach tightens a little at that. He has pulled some personal information out of me today. I opened up to him far more than I expected. He is, in fact, keeping up to his promise to get to know me before he kills me.

"I actually enjoyed this today," I say as I step into the living room. "You know, for not having much choice in my company."

"Do you really find me so offensive to be around?" he asks. But it's with mirth.

"I'm not going to further inflate your ego with a response," I say. I turn and head toward the stairs. "Good-night, Cyrus."

CHAPTER 9

I FEEL MY PHONE VIBRATE IN MY BACK POCKET, BUT MY hands are currently covered in make-up, spreading lipstick over Dora Lenard's lips.

Dora is an old woman. Ninety-eight years old. I already styled her snow-white hair. Dressed her in a simple but beautiful white gown that her family provided. Now I'm just finishing adding some blush to her cheeks, making her look a little more alive.

She died two days ago, on Tuesday. The family will bury her on Saturday, but Emmanuel, Craig, and Katie will take care of the service, giving me the weekend off.

I smile as I look down at her, satisfied that she looks great.

"You look beautiful, Dora," I say as I put the makeup away. "Just like you're ready for a night out on the town." I turn, putting things in their cabinet. "I know you. You were such a party animal. Nobody could talk you into turning it in early. You were always the life of the party."

I take my gloves off, throwing them in the trash.

"But all that changed when you met Brent," I say, standing beside her coffin, looking down at her peaceful face. "Then you only had eyes for him. Everyone made fun of you guys, but that's the story you guys stuck to." I smile. "Wouldn't that be nice? To have it be so easy?"

Love at first sight. Or really just any kind of love.

Everyone always talks about how teenage girls fall in love easily, how they fall for the wrong guys.

But I can honestly say I've never fallen for any guy.

I have no idea what love feels like.

"You look beautiful," I say once more, patting Dora on the arm, giving her a sad, maybe slightly jealous smile.

My phone vibrates again, reminding me that I had a text come through. I walk toward the lockers where my purse hangs, ready to head home, and pull it out.

Bring me another $1,000 a week from today.

My body instantly goes cold. My knees shake just slightly.

Payment isn't supposed to be due for another two weeks, I text back with shaking fingers.

Seven days, Shylock responds. Nothing more.

I look up, my eyes not really seeing anything as they scan the space.

I'm working long, crazy hours to earn the money to keep up with Shylock's demanding payment schedule. But this?

Pushing up the payment day by a week? There's no way I can have that money in time.

I swallow once, blinking five times fast, and shove my phone back into my pocket.

It's eight o'clock when I step out into the darkening evening. After four days of this, I hardly even notice when Mina steps out of the shadows and slips into my passenger seat.

My hands shake as they hold the steering wheel. I hardly even pay attention to where I'm going as I pull out onto the main road and head to the house.

I have five hundred, or rather I will have it by tomorrow. But payday won't be for another two weeks after that, long after Shylock's seven-day deadline.

Where am I going to come up with another five hundred?

I could sell my car. It's probably worth two thousand. But then how am I supposed to get to work to continue paying him off? I don't own anything else of value.

Borrowing it from my parents is out of the question. They'll ask what I need it for, and there's no way I'm dragging them into this mess.

The giant house looms up ahead, and I park in the last garage bay. Still completely ignoring Mina's presence, I walk inside.

I look around.

Everything in this house is nice. Expensive.

My eyes scan the lamps. The artwork on the walls. The pottery in the kitchen.

Could I resort to stealing something from this house and pawning it to get the money?

My jaw clenches.

To protect my family, to protect Amelia, from Shylock, yes, I could.

I'm so absorbed in my own neck-deep crap that I don't even realize I've stopped, frozen in the doorway between the mudroom and the kitchen.

Cyrus stands at the dining table, his hands braced on its surface, looking at me expectantly.

"Are you alright?" he asks, his brows furrowing.

I realize he's probably said something, but I didn't hear a word of it.

"Of course I'm not alright," I snap, defaulting to angry and pissed. "Everything in my world is wrecked and ruined and it's all your fault."

Cyrus' brows raise, his lips parting just slightly.

"The idea of coming home from work every day and having to check in just makes my stomach turn," I spit, crossing to the fridge and yanking it open. "But I can't even really be mad, because this is just how my life goes. Everything goes from bad to worse. Maybe I ought to just get it all over with now and let you kill me."

I grab a package of sliced meat and a block of cheese and slam the door shut.

To my surprise, Cyrus is standing just behind it, looking at me with concerned eyes.

"What happened today, Logan?" he asks.

I hate that his voice is so tender, so concerned.

The man is a psychopath. A kidnapper. A murderer.

But he sounds so genuine.

"Nothing out of my crappy usual," I mutter, turning away from him and working on my sandwich.

"I'll trade you problems," he says, arching an eyebrow.

"What's that supposed to mean?"

He turns, folding his arms over his chest. "I told you how one of the Houses in China was being a problem."

I nod, recalling what he said about rules, written and unspoken.

"And you understand that whatever age a human dies at their first death, they'll Resurrect and stay that same age for the rest of their immortal life."

"Yes," I say, trying to figure out where this is going.

"The Royals in China have seven children," Cyrus says, and his tone grows harder. "Apparently, there's been a feud between the two Houses in their country. It's been a game of size and power. But the House of Hou is not a patient one."

My brows furrow and my stomach feels sick. "How old are their children?"

He seems pleased, as if I figured this out quicker than he expected.

"They just turned their middle child," Cyrus says, his voice hardening. "A girl, who is barely eight years old."

My stomach twists. "No," I gape. "That's…that's sick. Now that poor girl is going to have to live the rest of her life, stuck in the body of an eight-year-old?"

Cyrus nods. He takes a step forward, his expression darkening. "You see, Logan. I wish I could make you understand that all these human problems you're dealing with, they are so temporary and insignificant for you," Cyrus says, standing just at my side, watching as I return to preparing my sandwich.

I want to bite back at his dismissal of my problems. But he's right. What I'm going through, compared to all these things he apparently has to deal with...

I slice the cheese, only I place the blade too high on the block and slice off a piece far too thick to use on a sandwich. Gently, Cyrus takes the blade from my hand, and begins slicing perfectly thin pieces.

"I need to make you see that what is waiting for you beyond your death is so much greater than everything you've experienced," he says, looking up to meet my eyes as he slides the cutting board in my direction. "Because right now, I can see that you still do not grasp any of it. You still cannot comprehend any scale of what is waiting for you."

His hands. The way he handles the knife. Such precision. Such control.

The breath is caught in my chest, and I don't even seem to care.

I watch Cyrus' lips as he speaks.

Those beguiling, enchanting lips.

"I am taking you to Las Vegas this weekend," Cyrus says, and my eyes flick up to his in surprise. "We will pay a visit to the House of Valdez. I want you to see what our world is really about."

Our world.

He says it with such ease.

Like he really believes it. Doesn't doubt it at all. Like it isn't so totally crazy.

"Fine. But first I need to go back to my apartment and clear out the rest of my things," I say, not letting him see the disbelief crawling all through my body. "Might as well wrap that up first. And you're coming to help me. You. Not Mina. Not Fredrick. So, pick me up after work tomorrow with a truck. And bring some work gloves."

Cyrus stares at me, emotionless, for a moment. But slowly, slowly enough that it creeps into my chest and wraps a razor net around my heart, a smile pulls on his mouth. He takes one step away from me, and then another.

I look over his shoulder, at Mina and Fredrick, who watch us. Each of them wears an equally shocked expression.

And I know, Cyrus is not the kind of person you boss around.

But I don't give a damn who he is to the rest of them. I'm not going to let him have all the control.

I'M DOUBTFUL.

Yes, I bossed Cyrus around. I told him he had to help me himself. But he's obviously a big wig. He might have looked entertained by my attempts to tell him what to do, but that doesn't mean he'll do it.

But when I walk out of Sykes Funeral Home at five o'clock, it's not Mina or Fredrick waiting inside a small moving truck. It is, in fact, Cyrus.

A little smile crooks in the corner of my mouth as I walk across the parking lot. I can't see his eyes, because they're covered with thick sunglasses, but a little smile of his own pulls on his lips.

"I'm surprised," I say when I pull the door open and slip into the passenger seat. "I didn't think you'd really be here."

"I'm a man of my word," he says. He puts the truck into gear, and with a jerky jump forward, he turns to leave the parking lot. "Look, I brought gloves and everything."

He nods his head toward two pairs of gloves on the dashboard. A larger black pair for him, and a smaller pink pair for me.

I huff a laugh and shake my head.

Ridiculous. All of it.

Cyrus still has a long way to go in becoming a smooth driver, but he gets us there without any damage to the truck, or anyone else on the road. He pulls into the parking lot of my apartment and backs toward my stairs, taking up two parking places.

Thankfully it's fairly quiet, most people still at work.

I climb out, digging through my purse for the keys. Up the stairs I climb, Cyrus only three steps behind.

I slow as I approach the door, and my heart sinks into my stomach as I see the lime green piece of paper taped to the door.

SECOND NOTICE OF EVICTION. ALL BELONGINGS WILL BE FORFITTED IN SEVEN DAYS.

I reach out to snatch it from the door, but another hand darts out, ripping it from the tape.

"Eviction?" Cyrus says, reading it over with furrowed brows. "On what grounds?"

My eyes dart over to his for just a moment. My jaw tightens.

I shove the key into the lock and push the door open.

"I've had a few financial problems in the last two months," I say simply, reaching for the light switch, only it doesn't flick the lights on.

Great. The power has been shut off.

"Did you know about this, before you brought me here today?" Cyrus asks, following me inside.

"Yes," I say emptily.

I immediately head toward my bedroom. I pause in the doorway, pulling out my phone. I text Amelia.

A few changes of plan. I'm finding a new place to stay. Think you could pick up the last of your things in the next week?

She responds immediately. *Oh, wow. Yeah, I'm just at Tanner's. I can be over there in about an hour.*

An hour?

I swear under my breath.

Great. There will be no avoiding a face to face.

I don't own hardly anything. But I really doubt that Cyrus and I will be done in an hour.

K, I respond. *See you soon.*

"Where would you like me to start?"

I turn around to see Cyrus surveying everything, a look of pity and slight disgust on his face.

He looks so out of place here. He's so regal, so sophisticated. But here he is, in my dumpy apartment.

"Let's get the big stuff loaded first," I say, looking around. "Half is mine, half Amelia's."

I'm grateful that Cyrus says very little as he helps me load the couch. The TV and stand. My dresser and bed.

Crap. My stuff is crap.

Now that I've lived in Cyrus' house for a while, I realize just how poor I am. How awful all my stuff is.

Why even keep any of my junk? I'll be living out the remainder of my human days with Cyrus.

But what about after?

I have no idea where I'll be expected to go after.

Cyrus loads my few dishes into boxes while I finish packing up all my things in the bathroom and my bedroom.

I find two pictures in the back of my closet. They're of me and Amelia our freshman year at Greendale Community. We'd snuck into this party. Greendale has no actual frats, but there was this one apartment building close to campus that tried to act like they were. It was so lame, we were laughing at all the thinly veiled attempts all the guys made to get us into bed.

We'd snapped pictures with all the drunk, passed out idiots we'd found, after we'd drawn mustaches on their faces.

I smile, remembering the fun, simple night. It had been exactly what I'd needed.

But I look around, to my now empty room, and realize,

there aren't going to be any more fun-filled, lighthearted nights for me.

"Lo?"

All my internal organs disappear at the sound of Amelia's voice.

"Oh, hi," I hear her say as I scramble to my feet. "You, uh, you must be Collin."

I dart out into the living room, just in time to see Cyrus walking toward Amelia, his hand outstretched.

"And you must be Amelia," he says with a charming smile.

Except charming doesn't even begin to cover it.

Through the terror ripping through my gut, it also fills with butterflies.

"I am," Amelia says, blushing, hard. She keeps giving him this little…look. Flirtatious, embarrassed, giddy. "It's nice to finally meet Logan's mystery man."

"Hey," I say. But my voice sounds too tight. Too strangled. "You sure got over here quick."

My beautiful, blonde bombshell friend looks over at me. "Well, yeah. You randomly say you're giving up the apartment and giving me a tight deadline put a little fire under me. What's the deal?"

I feel my face blanch. Think. Think, think, *think.*

"When Logan told me she was having a difficult time keeping up with the rent on her own, I offered her a room in my house." Cyrus offers a smooth, logical lie, just like that.

I look over at him. And I'm…grateful.

"Really?" Amelia asks doubtfully, looking between Cyrus and I. "You two are already moving in together?"

I bite my lower lip. I reach out for her hand. "Can…can I talk to you alone for a sec?"

Amelia glances back at Cyrus once more but follows me.

I pull her into my bedroom and shut the door. It's only a façade of privacy, I know Cyrus says he can hear every word. But I need Amelia to think this is just between the two of us.

"Lo, this seems a little crazy," she hisses, her voice low. "You've only know this guy for what? A week? You can't be serious about moving in with him!"

I have to sell this.

I have to make her believe this is for the best. Because I can't answer with the truth, to any of her questions.

"Look," I say, trying to seem a little embarrassed. "I didn't want to say anything because I didn't want you to feel bad. But covering all the rent on my own has been a little more challenging than I expected. You're right, it is way early in this thing to be moving in together. But Amelia, I'm happy."

Sell it.

Let it show in your eyes. Smile. Stand straight.

"Collin is…not like anyone I've ever met," I say. "You know me, I'm always so bitter that I just can't see past anyone's flaws. But Collin…" I pause, his face filling my mind. "He can take all of my acid. He's got his own special brand of it. And maybe this won't work out in the long run, but right now, this is where I am."

Whoa. I'm actually impressed with myself.

Amelia studies me, looking for signs of lies or distress.

But slowly, a smile creeps onto her face. She shakes her head. "It's about time you did something a little crazy and open up to someone." She laughs, throwing her arms around me. "I never expected this kind of speed from you, Lo. But I don't know. You just seem different. You got this, don't you?"

No. Not really. Not any of it.

Except for putting Cyrus in his place every now and then.

But I keep selling it.

I chuckle, squeezing her tight. "Thanks for understanding."

She lets go of me. "A week huh? And then we're out of here for good?"

I nod. And I'm filled with sadness.

"The end of an era." she says, frowning for show. "Look at us, growing up, getting in serious, committed relationships. We're hard core adulting these days."

I laugh. "Something like that." My eyes slide toward the door. "If you have a hard time getting ahold of me this weekend, don't freak, okay? Collin and I are taking a little trip this weekend."

"Again?" she asks, wagging her eyebrows. "You two are like animals. Where you headed this time?"

It'll be easier to keep my stories straight if I base them in truth. "Vegas."

This time, it's Amelia who blanches white faced. "Vegas? You're not... You're not going to go and elope on me, are you?"

A laugh bursts from my chest and I shake my head with a curse. "No, I swear it. I will not be returning from Vegas married to Collin."

She actually looks relieved. "You better not or I'm going to be seriously pissed. I claimed dibs on being your maid of honor years ago."

I smile, shaking my head, hugging her once more.

"I've really got to hurry," I say, releasing her. "Our flight leaves in three hours."

"Say no more," she says, flinging the door open and stepping out. "Have fun, but not too much fun."

She walks to the door. And I don't miss how she puts just a little more swing into her hips as she walks.

My face heats. My jaw clenches.

"Let's do a double when you crazy cats get back," she says, stopping in the doorway and turning back. "You two, and Tanner and I."

"I—" I go to decline.

"We'd be delighted," Cyrus cuts me off though, flashing another of those intense smiles.

Amelia winks at me, and then walks down the stairs to her car.

Slowly, I look over at Cyrus, glaring the look of death.

"It would have been rude to decline," he says, still smiling that wicked smile.

CHAPTER 10

WE DUMP MY LARGER THINGS AT A NEARBY STORAGE UNIT. IT hurts my pride when Cyrus pays for it, but I'm certainly in no position to say no. It's seven o'clock when we get back to the house.

I head to my room to pack, and for some reason, Cyrus follows me, watching as I sort through my clothes.

"You may bring a few casual clothes, but Mina has already packed you a bag with the essentials of what I would like you to wear." He walks into my room, standing just inside the doorway.

"What you would like me to wear?" I question, raising an angry eyebrow at him. "I know you're old, but this isn't the eighteenth century, anymore. You don't get to declare what you do and don't want me to wear."

There it is, that little gleam in Cyrus' eyes. Like a little thrill when I stand up to him. He takes two steps further into the room.

"Are you saying that you know what to wear when meeting the Royal family in Las Vegas? That you know what to wear to a ball hosted by vampires?"

I swallow. A chill tingles down my spine. A little fear. A little excitement.

My life may be insane right now. Chaotic. But it's gotten so much more interesting since Cyrus burst into it.

"Fine," I concede. I pull some shorts and a few t-shirts out and toss them into a bag. "Since I'm inexperienced in the political posturing events of vampires, I'll go with your suggestions."

"You are so kind," Cyrus banters.

"We need to leave now," Mina says from out in the hall.

I toss the rest of my things in my bag. And it's a little more than bizarre when Cyrus takes the bag from me, shouldering it without a word and walks down the hall.

The four of us load into the SUV and Fredrick drives us to the airport.

While I expected a domestic commercial flight at the Denver airport, we instead roll down an unfamiliar road, toward a further location from the main terminals. I look out the window, through the darkening evening, and my eyes widen slightly as Fredrick drives right up to a sleek white jet.

"Is this…" I stutter, watching the workers who hustle all around. "Is this yours?"

"When jet-setting around the world," Cyrus says as he opens the door, darting around to my side and opening mine,

"It's a much more pleasant experience when you have your own transportation."

I scoff, taking his hand as he helps me out. I shake my head, looking at the jet in disbelief.

The money this man must have. I can't even imagine what that must be like.

Fredrick and Mina take the bags, which there are quite a few of, and load them up into the plane. Cyrus stands at the bottom of the stairs, indicating a hand for me to take the stairs first.

A little bit of a smile pulls on my lips as I take them, one at a time.

I step inside, and it's just as luxurious as I imagined.

The entire interior is finished in black and white. The oversized seats are a plush white leather with black trim. The walls are darkest black, eating all the light. Red lights line the floor, casting a very faint glow.

"I hope you'll be comfortable for our trip," Cyrus' voice suddenly whispers next to my ear. I startle slightly, looking back at him. He wears an amused, satisfied smile.

The crew wraps things up, and Mina and Fredrick take seats toward the back, each on a phone, talking hurriedly to someone on the other end. Cyrus and I take seats on the same side of the plane, seats that face one another.

The pilot, a pale man with nearly white-blond hair comes out, speaking to everyone, but he says it in German. Cyrus quietly says something affirmative, and he disappears.

I look out into the dark while we taxi out onto the

runway. And just a minute later, I'm pressed back in my seat as we gain speed, and then, we're in the air.

"I wonder if you'll tell me," Cyrus says once we've finished climbing. "You've said some things that I don't quite understand. You seem to have had a good life. Loving parents. A younger brother you seem to care about. Rath, despite you not knowing the truth about him, has always been there for you. You're well on your way to your dream career." He pauses, studying me with his forest eyes. "But what you say. You called yourself bitter today when speaking to your friend. You said things go from bad to worse for you. Would you help me see where that comes from?"

He sits with one ankle over the opposite knee. His hand casually rests on his thigh, the other elbow braced in the window showing a dark world, slowly rubbing his chin.

Dark. Deep. Captivating. Terrifying.

He owns all of it.

I shake my head, looking back out the window. "You're very observant," I say. I tuck my knees up to my chest, wrapping my arms around them. "Life was going pretty good. I really shouldn't have anything to complain about. My parents are great. Eshan is a pest, but I love him. I have Amelia. Had Eli. And I love my job."

But I shake my head as I stare out at the night sky.

"Sometimes, even when you're doing everything right, life has a way of knocking you on your back, and kicking you while you're down."

My breath clouds the window, but I'm not really seeing anything.

"Money problems is the basic way to describe most of my downward spiral, but it's way more complicated than that," I breathe.

"I know it's of little comfort right now, Logan," Cyrus says quietly, "but once you step into your new life, money will never be of consequence again."

I look over at him. And I appreciate that he recognizes that it doesn't diminish the stress and pain it's caused me the last two years.

"I can take care of myself," I say. But it isn't stubborn or spitefully said. Just a stated fact. "I...I don't know how I'm going to figure this one out, but I always do."

He doesn't say anything for a long time, but I feel him watching me.

"What your friend said," he finally speaks. "What you said, that you've never been in love. Did you mean that?"

I look up. He really is observant.

"It's where it all started, the downward spiral," I say, being honest. "A month before I graduated from high school. I'd been dating this boy, Anderson, for two months." I shift, straightening, looking back outside. "I was trying to see what all the other girls were talking about. Trying to feel something for him. But no," I say. "It wasn't love."

"But something happened." His voice reveals the truth.

I nod. "He cheated on me. With one of my best friends. So, as you can imagine, it kind of wrecked the rest of the school year."

I hear a sound. Low. Rumbling. At first, I think it's the

plane. And then I realize it's coming from Cyrus. I look over to see the heat of embers rising in his eyes.

"I didn't care about losing Anderson," I say. "It was the sting of betrayal from one of my closest friends that hurt the worst. That's when I first learned to keep my circle small."

He nods, understanding.

"From there, it was just a series of unfortunate events, financially," I continue. "My dad made decent money as a contractor, but not enough to pay for my college. I worked my ass off the summer after graduating to earn enough for the first year of college. I made it, too. Everything I needed to pay for tuition, books, and most of my housing."

My fingers roll into little balls, my fingernails pressing sharply into my palms.

"I was on the way to the bank to deposit the second half of the money," I grit out. "I had to stop for gas, though. I'd run inside to pay with cash. But like an idiot, I forgot to lock the car."

"Someone stole half a year's worth of money," Cyrus fills in.

I nod. "I couldn't believe it. That it was just gone...all that time *wasted*. And that I could only pay for one semester. And I was too embarrassed to tell my parents what had happened. So, I just pretended that nothing had. I went to a bank to get a student loan."

My chest tightens, remembering the stress, the anxiety.

"The bank ran my credit. You don't need much of any to get a student loan. But when it came back, to them, it looked like I had over a hundred thousand dollars in debt to my name already."

"Identity theft," he once more predicts.

Once more, I nod. "Someone had stolen my identity six months prior and opened all kinds of accounts. The bank told me the sources to contact to work toward a resolution, but they couldn't loan me the money for school."

"What did you do?" Cyrus asks, shifting forward slightly.

My eyes snap over to him. "I took care of myself." My jaw clenches, to match the tightness in my chest. "And I keep taking care of myself. I'll keep doing it, until I can't."

I'm done talking.

And thankfully Cyrus gives me that.

ONLY TWO HOURS AFTER TAKING OFF, WE DESCEND INTO LAS Vegas. The lights really are mesmerizing. The sparkle. The busyness. Even from the air, I can feel the electric energy of the city.

The jet smoothly lands on the airstrip. Carefully, we taxi over to a slip and I hear the engines shut off, the plane cooling and settling.

Fredrick and Mina's voices softly cut through the plane. They frantically wrap up plans, arranging everything for our stay.

"Welcome to Las Vegas," Cyrus says. And I don't miss the little bitter edge to his voice.

I get the feeling he doesn't like this city.

The stairway opens and Fredrick and Mina exit first. Extending a hand for me to go ahead, I stand, and walk out the door.

The heat is suffocating.

Even though it's nearly midnight, the temperature must still be in the nineties.

A gigantic stretch limo waits before us. Black as night, it has to be three times longer than a normal SUV. And just as I step out onto the asphalt, one of the doors opens.

And out steps Edmond Valdez.

"Well, hello," he says, flashing a charming smile. "It's good to see you again."

My pulse immediately skyrockets. My palms sweat, and my wrists feel sore, as if bound by chains again. My hand rises to the side of my neck, where the woman who had been with him jabbed me with a needle, knocking me out for the night.

I knew we were coming to visit the House of Valdez. I wasn't prepared for the fear seeing this man would evoke in me again.

"Edmond," Cyrus acknowledges him, stepping forward. He places a hand at the small of my back, and oddly, it's comforting. "I hope you've had a pleasant evening thus far."

"It's been…busy," Edmond says, holding the door open for the limo.

I climb in, taking in the lavish interior of the space. More leather. Blue and purple lights. Bottles of what I assume is champagne. And something thicker, darker.

Everyone climbs inside, the doors slamming shut. Cyrus

slides up to my side, his thigh resting against mine, his shoulder pressing into mine in the tight space. The driver pulls forward.

"I've heard the House of Valdez has moved since I last visited," Cyrus says. He stretches out, resting his arm along the back of my seat. There's something…possessive, yet protective about it. Something that makes my stomach turn into a complicated knot.

"Yes, sir," Edmond says. And I realize. The way his eyes don't hold Cyrus' for very long. The way he bounces his left leg. That slight sheen of sweat on his upper lip. He's nervous. Incredibly so. "We're right in the heart of The Strip now. It makes operations easier."

"It's interesting, how some Houses prefer to operate in small towns, and others in large," Cyrus says. And he turns his head slightly, his eyes catching mine. "Your mother is based in a very small town there in Mississippi. The House of Sidra is right in the heart of Vancouver. Your cousin's House is right in the middle of Boston. Which was nearly their downfall."

We turn down a road and the lights become more intense. And even though it's late, even though it's been dark for hours, there are still so many people milling about outside.

"I, myself, prefer the slow and quiet," Cyrus says. His eyes also turn outside. "Too many people lead to the possibility of too many complications. There's a reason I have not visited Las Vegas in eighty-seven years. You cannot get a town more dissimilar to my home."

As if on planned cue, we turn onto another road, and The Strip opens up before us.

Lights blink. Lasers flash. Gigantic signs show images of near nudity and advertisements for magic shows.

Thousands of people crowd the sidewalks and car after car clogs the road.

Welcome to Sin City.

"Have you ever visited Las Vegas before?" Cyrus asks. His voice is low, intimate, meant just for me.

I nod. "Amelia and I took a road trip here last summer." I reflect, recalling the trip. "It wasn't what I thought it was going to be. I can't say I enjoyed it that much."

Cyrus doesn't respond, but as always, I know he's mulling over every word I say.

We drive two blocks, until we are indeed at the very heart of The Strip. And then we turn toward a massive building that glitters like silver under all the surrounding lights.

The MetroCosmo looks like something from the future. The entire building juts straight up and up, the windows and siding all one sleek sheet of silver, almost like a gigantic mirror reaching toward the sky.

The driver stops right in front of the giant doors. The doors to the SUV immediately open, and as I climb out, I see four workers, one for each door, and two that collect the baggage, loading it onto a cart.

Each of them bow to both Edmond and Cyrus.

My eyes slide over to Cyrus, and he just wears one of his little, mysterious smiles.

"Welcome to the House of Valdez," Edmond says, looking over his shoulder as he heads for the doors.

"Is…" my voice falters. "Is Eli…Rath, here?"

"Yes," Cyrus answers, watching as Mina and Fredrick fuss about, commanding the various employees to do this or that.

"Can I see him?" I ask.

"It depends." He slides his hands into the pockets of his expensive-looking jeans.

"On what?" I demand with annoyance.

"On whether or not you win the game."

The look in his eyes darkens. The coyness in his smile deepens.

And a drop of cold acid plunks in my stomach.

"What game?" I ask around a tight throat.

He loops an arm over my shoulders and steers us to the doors. "You'll see."

I shrug him off as I step through, but immediately stop dead.

The interior of the resort is heart stopping.

The ceiling soars above us. It stretches probably seven floors high. Suspended from the ceiling are mirrors. Long, thin. Round. Jagged and half broken. Mirrors of every shape and form hang down from the ceiling, looking almost as if they're suspended in mid-air.

And lights cut all around the space. Blue and purple lights bounce off the mirrors, casting light in every direction in a crazy laser grid.

It looks like we stepped right into the middle of a science fiction space bar.

It's stunning.

Breath taking.

"I'll admit," Cyrus breathes as we slowly walk inside, "as much as I dislike this city, the House of Valdez gives an impressive front."

Impressive doesn't begin to cover it.

Everyone milling about inside, playing at the game tables, sitting at the bars, lounging on expensive and massively large black couches, looks alien-like. Their skin glows blue and purple. Their eyes seem too shiny and bright. Teeth glow and I'm searching for fangs but see none.

"Are they all vampires?" I breathe as I follow the crew from the limo into the heart of the casino.

"No," Cyrus says, and I see his nostrils flare slightly as he takes in a deep breath. "Some, but not most. The casino functions as any other on The Strip, but it is the House that owns and runs it."

"We occupy the top three floors of the building." Edmond's voice cuts through the crowd, and we suddenly stop at a wall that looks just like a big mirror. He places his hand on it and a beam of light flashes underneath it. "But the rest of the casino is just like any other. Though, if you pass out drunk here, you may wake up with a sore neck, and feeling slightly lightheaded."

My stomach flips and my eyes slide to Cyrus', searching for confirmation. He only gives a slight nod.

Cyrus said the point of this trip was to make the reality of his world real to me.

It's working.

The wall suddenly opens, revealing an enormous elevator. With Cyrus' hand once more at the small of my back, we all step forward and inside.

The doors shut when Edmond presses a button.

This is no normal elevator. We immediately shoot upward, at an insane speed. My knees buckle at the unexpected thrust.

Instantly, Cyrus' arm wraps around my waist, pulling me against him to keep me upright.

I meet his eyes for a long moment, and he stares at me.

Cyrus has a face you could get lost in for hours. The most powerful gaze you'd ever meet. Penetrating. Probing.

But I can feel a dozen more eyes watching us. And sure enough. I look around, and see every single person in this elevator looking at the two of us, almost expectantly. Perhaps hopefully.

I don't understand a single bit of that.

All too soon for how tall I know the building is, the elevator slows and then stops. The big doors slide open.

And once more I'm stunned.

Enormous windows, with seemingly no walls to brace them, open up the view over the city.

Black floors, black walls, and black ceiling tunnel my view and without encouragement, I step forward, heading toward that window.

The MetroCosmo must be the tallest building on The

Strip. Nothing towers over my view. Lights and buildings and glistening darkness reflect back at me and take my breath away.

"It is stunning in its own, modern way."

Cyrus' voice cuts through my enchantment. He stands beside me, looking out at the view with me.

I just nod.

"If you'll follow me," Edmond's voice interrupts, "I'll show you to your suite."

Cyrus reaches for me, pulling me along beside him.

Edmond shows us down a hall, all lined with black on the floor and ceiling. But the walls, they all appear to be mirrors.

Edmond stops somewhere a little ways down the hall. He nods his head to Cyrus, who is smarter than I am and figures it out. He raises his hand, placing it on the mirror. And a set of double doors slide open.

"Per your request, the family will greet you in the morning," Edmond says as Cyrus and I step inside. He bows deeply, and turns to leave.

The door slides closed behind him.

As with the rest of the resort, all the walls inside are mirrors. A sitting room occupies the center. The ceiling rises high, and from it hangs a chandelier of mirrors and blue and purple lights. Black furniture is arranged in a circle.

Off to the left and right, there are doors opening to bedrooms, furnished in a similar manner.

Straight ahead is another wall of windows, granting a different view of the city.

Impressive.

"I thought you might like some rest before everything begins," Cyrus says.

He stands directly beneath the chandelier, watching me as I walk around, taking it all in.

"You really think I'll sleep with everything that's already going on?" I scoff.

"I suggest you try," he says.

Movement to my left draws my eye to one of the bedrooms.

A woman steps into view. Blonde hair, heavily made up face, thin figure. She wears a simple, tight-fitting black dress.

She steps forward, waiting in the doorway.

"Who…" I trail off, watching as Cyrus steps forward. Red embers ignite in his eyes.

"Get some sleep, Logan," he says without looking back at me. "I really don't think you want to watch this."

And my eyes grow wide in horror, a gasp rips from my throat.

The moment Cyrus reaches the woman, he sinks fangs into her neck. He walks them back a step into the room, and pushes the mirrored doors closed behind him.

CHAPTER 11

BLOOD. FANGS. RED EYES.

Vampire.

Vampire.

Vampire.

Cyrus is a vampire.

Edmond is a vampire.

Mina, Fredrick.

All vampires.

And Cyrus is one hundred percent sure that I will be one some day, too.

But how can I believe him? How can I be one hundred percent sure? Cyrus says I have to die, but what if that's it? What if he's wrong, and I don't wake back up after four days like he says?

And then what?

I'll have to live here at one of the Houses? I'll drink

blood and lose all my humanity? Because, so far, none of the ones I have met seem to have much of it.

Fitfully, I toss and turn in my larger than king sized bed. When I do sleep, my dreams are full of fangs. Full of cold castles. Filled with faces and faces and never-ending generations of child vampires.

I'm plagued by my own thoughts all throughout the night.

When dawn finally crests through the open window in my bedroom, I'm exhausted. But relieved.

It's time to deal with my reality.

I drag myself from the bed and head into the ornate and massive bathroom. Inside, I find an outfit hanging, ready for me to put on.

If they're going to be picky and judgmental about what I wear, I'm going to own it.

I shower. I dry my long, dark hair and style it into a severe and complicated up-do. I go heavy and dark with my makeup.

Then I slip into the black pencil skirt. Red stitching outlines every feature. I pull on the top, thin, nearly sheer white fabric with a complicated lace overlay that shows off my shoulders and is open down the middle of my back.

I look at myself in the mirror.

I look terrifying. Like I could command the world to crumble and it would obey.

Filled to the brim with confidence, overflowing with determination, I walk across my bedroom, and throw the doors open.

For some reason, I expected Cyrus to be standing there, waiting for me.

So, when it's Mina standing there, I stop in my tracks.

"The Royal family is waiting for you," she says with her heavy accent.

Without waiting for me to catch up to speed, she turns, and walks out of the suite.

I notice that the windows that once granted such a spectacular view of the city last night, are no longer anywhere to be found. Where they once were, there are now only mirrored walls.

I follow, taking care not to trip in my high heels.

She guides us back to the elevator, and then we rise up, but not for long. It slows, and opens back up.

It immediately reveals a massive space. A wide-open ballroom with black floors and black walls. The roof rises high. High enough I only see black above us. And hanging from the ceiling, there are four gigantic mirrored chandeliers.

Every bit of the House of Valdez has been dazzling and overwhelming. I'm constantly looking all around me, in awe.

So, it takes a moment before I even notice the line of people across the great hall.

Mina's hand pushes against my back, urging me forward.

Own this, I think to myself. *If they're going to make you completely change your life, don't be afraid. Show them that you won't be cowed.*

My heels click over the stone floor, echoing through the massive room.

It's large enough it takes a dozen or so steps before I can recognize who all I am looking at.

People, a few faces I recognize, most I don't, stare at me. They're dressed in finery. Mostly black. They stare me down with watchful eyes. Each and every one of them silent.

But it's Cyrus that I can't look away from as I cross the room. It's his black suit with red stitching that matches my skirt that commands respect. It's his penetrating gaze and mirthful little smile in one corner of his mouth that I can't quite look away from.

But it's the throne he sits upon, and the crown atop his head, that steels my breath.

I slow as I approach it—him, and the others. And come to stand before the man who commands power. The man who radiates strength and instills fear in the eyes of vampires.

And I know.

I understand now.

"Your Majesty," I say, taking a bow, letting my eyes fall from his. I repeat those words I heard from Edmond, two weeks ago, but did not comprehend at the time.

Cyrus, I think as I straighten, *is King.*

"Hello, Logan," he says, still holding that little smile. He always seems too amused, watching us little pawns scurry around for his game. He admitted to it before, he stated it last night.

"I always said you were someone important," I say, forcing my voice not to shake. "But I think I was in denial that I was being held captive by a king."

A darkness flickers through Cyrus' eyes at that word. His smile falters just a bit.

"Now you see why I am so involved in the affairs of the Houses," he says as he stands. He slowly crosses toward me. My eyes rise to the crown atop his head. It's simple, really. Only solid gold. But it's scarred, stained. The sharp points of it that circle his head show signs of war and wear. "One must know everything if one is to rule them all."

I meet his deep eyes. "Either that, or you're just plain controlling."

A sharp intake of breath echoes throughout the hall. That's when my heart jumps into my throat, fear ripping through my veins. I look over Cyrus' shoulder to see everyone behind with shocked expressions on their faces.

But as I look back at Cyrus, he only smiles that smile of his.

"There's something about you, Logan Pierce," he says smoothly. "That is for certain."

Everyone is deadly quiet. As if they're waiting for something. For backlash. For him to strike me down.

But Cyrus only takes my hand, and turns back to the crowd. Taking his lead, I step four steps forward, side by side with him.

"To the honorable House of Valdez," he says, his voice booming with power. "I present Logan Pierce, daughter of Alivia Conrath. Descendant of my grandsons, Dorian *and* Malachi."

Another reaction of awe and shock.

My grandsons?

What…what does that even mean?

There are so many things that I could question from just those two words.

But right now, everything, *everything* is about showing no fear.

Only projecting confidence.

A man steps forward. He looks maybe thirty, at most. As I study him, I pick out similarities. Edmond's same eyes. Same chin.

"Logan, I'd like to introduce you to Hector Valdez, the leader of the House of Valdez," Cyrus presents the man, who extends a hand. I take it, shaking his firm grasp.

"It is a surprise to meet you," he admits honestly. "And the rumors are true. You look just like your mother. She was here at my House just a few years ago."

This. This is the part that I am not prepared for.

That there is all this history. All these people connected to a mother who I know nothing about.

"As I have heard," I say, because it's the only thing that comes to mind.

"As our newest Royal, I hope you have a pleasant visit to the House of Valdez." He smiles, though it's tight. And I see it, same as on Edmond last night: he's nervous.

"You have met my youngest son," Hector says, turning slightly, extending a hand toward Edmond. "My middle son, Horatio, has lived at Court for some years now. And this is my eldest son, Rafael." He holds his hand out, in the other direction.

A beautiful man, who looks very similar to his younger

brother, steps forward. He takes my hand, cupping it with the other. He presses a kiss to my knuckles. "It is a pleasure to make your acquaintance."

He looks up at me through thick eyelashes. And something tingles in my lower belly.

A low rumble resonates from Cyrus, and I look over at him to see red embers ignited in his eyes.

Rafael immediately drops my hand, and steps back into line.

Cyrus is certainly intimidating and scary. But I'm getting the feeling I don't know a hundredth of it.

"And this is the rest of my House," Hector says, turning and waving a hand to the—I quickly count—twenty-four other people standing on this side of the hall. "There are others, but they are out doing their duties."

Jobs. Duties. It's hard to grasp when I know every one of them is a blood-sucking vampire.

"It's a pleasure to meet you all," I say, though my voice is not as loud as I would have liked it.

Hector nods his head slightly. "Your highness, for your entertainment, I present our upcoming show, Sands of Set."

A door opens to the right of the hall, and eerie and foreign music flutters through the huge space. Pulsing. Powerful.

Through it, walk a dozen women. They wear harem pants with intricate designs, scanty tops, scarves wrapped around their faces. Glittering jewels hang from their costumes.

They move and dance as they proceed into the hall.

I look to see Cyrus' reaction to the sultry procession.

His face is blank.

He reaches for my hand and he guides us back to his throne. He indicates the seat beside his, nearly as ornate as his own, and sits.

He leans back in his seat, one ankle crossed over a knee. He laces his fingers together across his chest.

And from under that crown, upon his throne, the King watches the show.

The women are talented. There is no doubt about that. They roll and writhe, twisting their hips in incredible movements. Their hands dance, fluttering about like they're riding a wind.

It's memorizing. There's something ancient and primal about their movements, and as I watch, I realize they're actually telling a story. A story about a queen, revered and loved. A woman with power, but a woman who was kind and great.

And then lost.

A single dancer flutters around the room, the others sliding into shadow. She willows in and out of the dark. And with a dramatic, sharp movement, she suddenly drops to the ground, as if dead.

The music stills, becomes a thrumming pulse.

Long, heavy, dramatic moments pass, and she does not move.

Cyrus' breathing grows harder.

I look over at him.

His jaw is clenched hard. His nostrils flare slightly. His left hand grips the armrest of his throne hard, and I see the metal bending under his strength.

The music reaches a dramatic peak. The woman on the floor slowly climbs to her feet.

She looks around as if lost. Confused.

I realize that Cyrus is holding his breath.

And his mouth hangs just so slightly open.

His eyes have ignited a brilliant red. Black veins creep from around his eyes, stretching out over his face. But there, I see just a tiny bit of emotion welling in them.

"Stop this!"

The words rip from my lips before I even give them a second of consideration as to what I am saying.

The woman—the queen, the dancer—instantly stills, looking at me with surprised, fearful eyes. The music cuts off, and every eye turns to me.

I look at Cyrus, but he only stares at the dancer with unrelenting focus.

"I'm bored to tears," I lie, but put every ounce of confidence I have into my voice. "If this is your King, I suggest you come up with something better."

"Excuse *me*," Hector says, stepping forward. "This is not for you to evaluate or to dismiss. I don't know who you think you are-"

"Get out," Cyrus suddenly says. His voice is low. Dangerous.

"Your Majesty-" Hector begins to say.

"I said get out!" Cyrus suddenly bellows. That emotion I saw in his eyes, it's hidden now, but I can still interpret the pain there. "The woman said she did not like your show, and so I command you to take it elsewhere, and yourselves with it."

Every one of these vampires, these Royal and powerful vampires, looks at Cyrus with absolute terror. They tremble.

"I shall summon you, Hector, once I have consoled poor Logan," Cyrus says. "For her utter disappointment in the woeful entertainment you who call yourselves Royals have provided. Prepare to participate in some *real* entertainment when I do."

Cyrus' voice grows more dangerous with every word spoken.

The color disappears from every face around us with his last sentence.

"Go," Cyrus says quietly.

They all finally move. Some of them dart out of the hall, so fast they're nothing more than a blur. But the Royal family; Hector, Rafael, and Edmond, slowly walk toward the elevator. Edmond looks over his shoulder as they go, meeting my eyes.

And I swear I see utter hatred in them. A promise of revenge.

A tingle rushes over my skin. Fear. Exhilaration. The promise of a challenge.

Who am I these days?

The hall empties, leaving Cyrus and I alone in silence.

I don't know what to say. I don't know what to do now.

Cyrus stares at that place where the dancer stood just moments ago.

"Thank you," he whispers, his voice hoarse.

My throat is tight. "You're welcome," I manage.

We sit there for several long moments. The silence is heavy. Suffocating. Filled with too much…just too much.

I press my hands together, tucking them between my knees, unsure what to do with myself.

"Do you want to be alone?" I ask.

He doesn't answer immediately, and I get the impression he's debating the question. "Yes."

I don't know what makes me extend the mercy, but I reach out, placing my hand on his forearm.

I don't know what about the dancers brought out such emotion. But his pain—it's so tangible I can nearly touch it.

His eyes shift over to my hand. When he doesn't say anything more, I stand. With my heels clicking over the marble floor, I walk to the elevator. It opens as soon as I stand in front of it.

I step inside, not looking back at the king.

And just as the doors slide closed, I hear a howl of agony rip between captivating lips.

The elevator goes down two floors, and when it opens, it's to the common room from last night. But now, all the windows overlooking the city are mirrors. And it's packed full of people.

Yelling, arguing, worried words fill the air.

But the second I step out, they all fall dead silent. Every single pair of eyes slides to me.

Hector looks worried, but ready to fight. Edmond looks prepared to kill. Rafael just seems uncertain.

Mina and Fredrick seem almost smug. Like they know what is to come.

"He's going to begin a game, isn't he?" Hector asks. And the way his voice shakes, I understand there is history here.

Game. I see a pattern rising. The King himself has said the words. Now they come from a House leader.

"I don't know what that dance up there was," I say, keeping my voice cool and calm, "but I do know that you all have been under Cyrus' rule for quite some time. I know that you should have known better."

Mixed emotions fill faces around me. Shame. Acceptance. Surprise. Confusion.

"Whatever comes after this," I say as I step forward, "you all asked for it."

Through a crowd of vampires, I walk, parting them as I go. I don't look back as I make my way to my suite.

A moment of silence follows me. But then there are whispers. Hurried. Excited. Fearful.

There's not a doubt in me that they are about me.

I place my hand on the mirror wall and my doors pop open. I walk inside, closed into the silence of our rooms.

The windows here are open. I walk to them, looking out over the day casting light on the city.

Yet all I really see are those tears pooling in Cyrus' eyes.

CHAPTER 12

Two hours later, the door to my suite opens. Mina walks in with a knowing, dark smile.

"The King is ready for you again," she says. And there's a dangerous glint in her eyes that tells me something big is about to happen.

She crosses to my closet, throwing it open. She comes out carrying a long garment bag. "He requests that you change into this." She hands it over and heads for the door. "I shall wait for you outside."

Slowly, I zip the bag open, my eyes growing wide as I take in the new outfit.

Ten minutes later, because it's not the easiest thing to change into, I walk out of the suite in my newest dress.

It's made of soft black leather. A deep plunging neckline exposes more cleavage than I'm used to. Straps and buckles crisscross over my hips, across my back. It stretches long to the floor.

I look like the goddess of war.

With an approving smile, Mina leads us to the elevator. Instead of rising up again, we go down. Plummeting in this speedy elevator, we dive through the belly of the MetroCosmo.

When the doors slide open, it's to a nearly pitch-black hallway. Only faint blue lights line the floor, dimly guiding us forward.

There are roped lines leading up to doors, suggesting wherever we are headed is used frequently for events.

This is Vegas. And each casino has a showroom.

Perhaps this is where *Sands of Set* will be regularly performing.

Mina opens a door and I step inside.

It's an arena. A huge stage is set below me, circled entirely by seats. The entire space is illuminated by gold and red lights. The thrones from upstairs have been moved down here, placed just on the edge of the stage.

There's no one else here.

Carefully, so as to not trip, I descend the stairs.

Just as I step onto the stage, doors open from off to the right, and in files the House of Valdez.

They wear…costumes. Each of them is dressed like someone from an ancient time. Leather skirts with straps that look meant to hold weapons. They look like…gladiators.

From the shadows, a figure walks up to the stage. The lights glint off of a crown, and Cyrus steps into view.

"I do not enjoy the city of Las Vegas," he says. His voice is low. Dangerous. He looks out at the House of Valdez, his eyes dark. He goes to stand in front of his throne. "It stinks of sin and deceit. It never grows dark. It never knows quiet. It races too fast, trying to be too modern."

The room is deathly quiet, waiting to hear what their King has in store for them.

"It makes me long for a simpler time," Cyrus says. The faintest tick of a smile pulls on the corner of his mouth. "A time when offenses were settled with iron and blood. A time of brutal entertainment. Oh, how I miss those days."

He snaps his fingers and four men enter through the doors to the right. They're burly, built. They carry large wooden crates. Without hesitating, they march up to the stage and set the crates down.

In them is an arsenal of weaponry. Shining iron. Spiked ore.

"It has been some time since I have enjoyed an old-fash-ioned gladiator fight," Cyrus says. He extends a hand toward me, inviting me to his side. I go, but my heart rate spikes. "And while we shall not fight to the death, we shall fight to the last man standing. And the victor shall enjoy a dance with this enchanting young woman at the ball tomorrow."

My eyes widen but I keep as quick control as I can.

I am the prize?

One dance. To the victor of the last vampire standing?

As I look around, I see that each of them doesn't see this as much of a prize, either. But I also know, they don't have a choice in this.

This is King Cyrus' entertainment. This is his punishment for what happened earlier.

"As House leader, I shall let you pick the opponents," Cyrus says. "This will be a single elimination event, until our final two contestants. And everyone," he turns his eyes to Hector, Rafael, and Edmond, "must participate."

I hear the faint muttering of protest from some of the House members, but Edmond raises a hand, and they immediately fall silent.

"Pick your first two opponents," Cyrus says darkly. He turns and crosses to his seat.

Slowly, I follow him, sinking into the seat beside him.

"Are you all right?" I quietly breathe without looking over at him.

Instead of answering, Cyrus extends his hand, scooping up mine. Without looking at me, he raises it to his lips and presses a kiss to my knuckles.

Another silent *thank you*. An admission that no, he is not all right.

The crowd clears from the stage, leaving only two people behind. A man, tall and skinny, and a woman, tall and built. They each wield a sword.

A cold sweat breaks out across my skin. My stomach feels as if it dissolves inside of me.

This is real.

Those are sharp blades. This is an arena.

And there will be blood spilt.

"Fight!" Cyrus bellows.

Both of the contestants rush forward, swinging their blades.

The woman immediately connects with the man's arm. I watch as if in slow motion, as it slices cleanly through his flesh. There isn't even time for the blood to spill before the blade hits bone, and as if made of steel, the blade bounces back.

The man gives a roar of pain, clasping his hand to his arm as blood gushes from the wound. Feebly, he darts to the other side of the arena, no more than a blur, but the woman is instantly there in front of him, dealing another crushing blow. He staggers back, his eyes igniting bright red.

The woman raises a foot and kicks it hard into his chest.

He sails across the arena, skidding on his back. A wheezing sound comes across his lips, his head knocking backward, hard against the floor.

The woman raises her hands in the air, declaring herself the victor.

The last man standing.

I understand the rule now. The first to fall to the ground is eliminated.

I look over to Cyrus to see him leaning forward, a wicked gleam in his eye.

I told them they would deserve whatever punishment he gave them, for causing him so much grief and pain earlier. Was that a mistake? Was I wrong? Because I certainly didn't understand the levels of brutality the man beside me would result to.

The next opponents step onto the bloodied stage. Two men, both huge in stature. Both with glowing red eyes.

"Fight!" Cyrus declares.

They rush forward, swords swinging.

Blood splatters onto the stage as they each take blow after blow. It's incredible to watch, really. They move with such speed at times I can hardly even tell where they are. And they both take strikes that would lob human limbs from bodies, over and over.

Bloodied and weak, one of the men slips to his knee. And it's a fatal mistake. He looks up at his opponent, just in time for him to swing a punch into his face.

The man sails back, landing flat on his back.

A cheer from the crowd sounds from a woman and another man.

I'm trying to understand the Houses. It seems they at least live in close proximity. I know from what Cyrus has said that at least some of them marry one another. They even have children sometimes. I would think they would be like family.

But these people, they swing swords at one another, and the look in their eyes, I swear, they really would kill one another to win. Even though there is no real prize.

"Do they not like each other?" I ask as the next set of opponents step up. "It certainly doesn't look like it. If they'd just as soon kill each other, why do they all live with each other?"

Cyrus smiles as he watches the blood spray across the stage. "Each House has its own politics and inner workings.

Some Houses band together for financial reasons. Like the House of Sidra." The women on the stage pummel one another. "Others evolve out of manipulation, like your mother's."

I internally recoil at that.

"And others simply like to be associated with power," Cyrus continues. "Like the House of Valdez. This is business and competition."

A woman collapses to the ground after an exceptionally hard blow. She's out.

"None of them are family, then?" I ask, disgust settling into my stomach. "None of them really care about each other?"

Cyrus' eyes flick over to mine and he takes me in. "Just because there is money, manipulation, competition, doesn't mean they aren't family. What family is perfect?"

The next competition is over in one perfect blow that sends the man flat on his face.

Family. This is nothing what my family looks like. Nothing like what I envisioned my future family to look like.

By the time the first round ends, there isn't a single inch of the stage that isn't covered in blood. The losers sit on one side of the arena, bandaging wounds, hissing and groaning and casting dark looks at their King.

For hours, the fights continue.

A fist meets a face, the hit so fierce that a spray of blood splashes me across the face. Flecks of it spatter across Cyrus' neck.

I was wrong before.

They don't deserve this.

Cyrus is enjoying it far too much.

But he is the King of vampires, and I am just a little, human girl.

I can feel it, as the sunsets and the hour grows late. I'm tired, exhausted. But finally, the final two contestants step onto the stage. Edmond, and a man with long blond hair and a wicked scar down his face. Bloody. Battered. Exhausted.

They ready themselves. And even though they're exhausted, I see the preparation in their eyes.

"To the last man standing," Cyrus hisses.

Edmond takes the first swing, though the other man quickly deflects it, spinning with impossible speed, taking a swing at Edmond's side, and landing.

The thud of metal on bone cracks through the arena.

Edmond twists, ducking low, kicking a leg out. The other man stumbles but with lightning speed, briefly puts some distance between the two of them.

On. And on. And on, they battle.

They are both covered in blood from head to foot. It drips down into their eyes, coats their teeth. They slip on the stage.

They are equally matched. And this could go on all night.

My fingers curl around the armrests. My jaw clenches. My blood boils too hot.

"That is *enough*, Cyrus," I say. Not loudly. But with finality. "You've punished them enough. You have taken this too far. End this. Now."

Every eye turns to me. Edmond and his opponent pause, though neither lowers their weapon.

They all keep looking at me like that. With shock. And maybe a little bit of reverence.

I look over at Cyrus, and slowly he looks back at me.

"I can't take another second of it," I say, looking at him with stone cold eyes. "The fact that you are enjoying this so much makes me sick."

Dead. Silence.

Not a one of them breathes. No one moves a muscle.

I feel their eyes shift from me, to Cyrus, and back to me.

Cyrus stands but never once takes his eyes from me. He reaches out, taking my hand and pulls me to my feet.

Fear. I should be feeling fear. Being touched by the man who brought about so much violence without anyone questioning him.

But all I feel is determination.

"You are all dismissed," Cyrus says, though hardly loudly enough for the giant space.

But one by one, they breathe in relief. They slowly trickle out that door.

Cyrus never once looks away from me though, never is distracted.

I raise my chin, determined not to cower under his penetrating stare. The House of Valdez might bow under his commands, but I am not one of them.

As the room empties, Cyrus looks at my hand. He turns it over, as if studying every inch of my skin.

"It has been a very, very long time since I have met anyone like you, Logan," he breathes. His thumb brushes over the center of my wrist. "Someone who does not recoil when in my presence. Someone who dares speak their mind."

He raises my hand, and brings his nose to trail along the inside of my wrist, slowly up the inside of my arm toward my elbow. His eyes slide closed as he slowly inhales.

There's something wrong with my heart. It flutters. It stops. It sprints.

My stomach is full of fluttering beasts.

"I told you that I would give you four weeks to finish your human life," he says, brushing his cheek along my skin. "I told you I am a man of my word." Every one of his words sounds pained, full of absolute longing. "But Logan, please, I beg of you. Please do not make me wait."

His voice actually cracks just slightly on his last sentence.

The agony in his words… A fracture splits in my chest and my breath catches.

"Why do you want me to die?" I ask. I raise my other hand and palm the side of his face. He presses it into my hand, still not opening his eyes. "Cyrus, what do you want from me?"

A pained breath rips from his chest and he turns to press his lips into my palm, cupping his hands around mine so that it does not escape.

Violent tingles spark in my lower stomach. I'm hardly breathing.

I can't look away from Cyrus' lips pressed against my palm. And I realize, I don't want him to pull them away.

"I am so tired of waiting," he whispers. He trails his lips, not kissing, just brushing them lightly against my skin, down to my wrist. "I've been so ready..." He continues dragging his lips along my arm. As he slides them up my bicep, it parts his lips and my body sparks in desire. I let my eyes slide closed just a little bit.

One of his hands wraps around my waist, pulling me closer. And slowly, slowly, those captivating lips of his slide across my shoulder, and rest against my neck.

"Please, Logan," he begs.

And instantly I come back to my senses as I feel the tiniest prick of pain against my flesh.

Fangs.

At my neck.

Ready to end me.

"No," I whisper, suddenly trembling.

I'm so confused. So conflicted. It's agony, it takes everything I have in me to take half a step back. Cyrus' eyes are foggy when they rise to meet mine. Filled with desire and lust and something I swear is love. But it can't be love because...because it's just impossible.

I shake my head. "There's still so much I have to finish. Still too much I have to learn. Still far too much I don't know about my future."

Slowly, the pain returns to Cyrus' face, and I think I die a little inside at the sight of it.

"Not yet," I say quietly.

But the pain turns to sadness and resolve. He nods as his shoulders sag in defeat. He turns to go.

"Did I win?" I ask quietly.

"Win?" he says, pausing.

"The game," I say. "You said I could see Eli if I won."

There's a little look of betrayal in his eyes that shatters my complicated heart.

"Yes," he says, sounding tired as the ocean. "You won. You may visit Rath, just for a few minutes."

Without another word and without any more begging, he turns, and walks out of the arena.

CHAPTER 13

I RETURN TO MY ROOM AND CHANGE. IT'S COMFORTING wearing my own clothes once more. Just simple shorts, and normal t-shirt. Even though my entire world has been turned upside down. Even though my insides are all inside out.

It's Rafael who waits for me outside my suite. To my utter shock, he looks perfectly normal once more, wearing clean clothes, no signs of blood, and no cuts all over his body.

"Vampires heal quickly?" I ask as I follow him to the elevator. I stand beside him uncomfortably.

"Yes," he answers stiffly. I have a feeling the King growling at him earlier has put him on edge when it comes to his interactions with me. "Even more so with the aid of human blood."

"Oh," is all I say around the tightness in my throat.

We plummet through the belly of the casino. Down and down until surely we're below ground level. Finally, the elevator slows, and then the doors open.

It's nearly pitch black as we step out. It's a long hall and only a single light is on the wall at the far end of it, probably fifty yards away.

Down the dim hall, I follow Rafael.

He walks to the middle of the hall and produces a set of keys. He unlocks a door, and holds it open for me.

A rush of cold air brushes over my skin as I step inside. If possible, it's even darker in here. I barely make out the shape of stairs descending down into roughly carved earth.

Down and down we walk, until finally we hit level ground.

It's a dungeon.

The space that opens up isn't particularly large. There are five prison cells that break off from the central space. A man sits in a chair in one corner, but darts to his feet when he sees us.

"Take a five minute break, Harris," Rafael says.

The man nods and sets up the stairs.

"Logan?"

Through the dark, my eyes search. They land on the furthest cell.

Eli climbs up from the ground, grabbing the bars.

"I'll just be at the top of the stairs," Rafael says, tucking the keys into his pocket. "Not that you can, but don't try anything." He turns and walks back up the stairs, leaving Eli and I alone.

Hesitantly, I take a step forward.

"Why are you here, Logan?" Eli asks. His voice is concerned, confused.

"Cyrus...the...the King," I say. My thoughts are a swirling, racing, confused mess. "He wanted me to understand. To show me what all of this...what it really means."

He shakes his head, letting it drop. "I'm so sorry, Logan. This shouldn't have happened. It should have been so much further down the road. I failed you, and I'm sorry."

I finish crossing to the cell, grabbing one of the bars. "What...what does that mean? Eli...Cyrus has said these things, and now, I don't think I really even know who you are."

Eli looks up, and there's pain and regret written all over his face.

"I was sent to Colorado sixteen years ago," he says. He hesitates, and I can see him debating this, telling me the truth. But he swallows once and then says, "By your mother."

My brows furrow and my hands are ice cold.

"She wanted to protect you," he says. Something softens in his voice when he speaks about my mother. "She knew that one day Cyrus would go looking for you, would find you, but she sent me, so that I could delay that day for as long as possible. And I failed. I am so, so sorry, Logan."

"Why?" I whisper. "Why would she think Cyrus would come looking for me? Cyrus is crazy and scary, but why would she be so worried about him finding me?"

Rath, because I realize now, that's who he's always really been—this entire time—shakes his head and lets it fall once more. "It doesn't…it doesn't even matter now. You'll die, and everything you were will probably be gone and your mother and I will just have to accept it."

My chest hurts. And I'm angry. I feel betrayed.

"None of that makes any sense," I say through clenched teeth. "Everyone just keeps speaking in riddles, being vague and so damn mysterious." I smack the bar in my frustration, but all it does is hurt my hand. I turn away so he won't see the angry tears rushing into my eyes.

"I want to protect you from this life for as long as I can," he says, resolved. Even he hardly believes his words. "To keep that weight from your shoulders until the last possible moment."

I shake my head, as one of the tears breaks free. I wipe at it angrily.

"I've thought of you as family for years, now," I say. "You were always there. Always had my back. Were always so caring." My voice grows hoarse. "But it was all a lie. Family doesn't keep secrets. Especially not of this scale."

His mouth opens and closes, but still, he won't tell me the truth.

"You know," I hiss. "You know exactly what is going on. But you keep your mouth shut. You keep Cyrus' secrets. You keep Alivia's secrets. You just let me run around with the King, looking like a complete fool."

I turn and head toward those stairs.

"Cyrus will kill me," I say, pausing. "He's incredibly anxious to do so. So, you'll be released, I promise. But I can tell you this." I hesitate, because the words are going to break me. "I won't bother you anymore once you're out. I realize now that sometimes you can't even trust those closest to you. You can't trust someone you don't even know."

I turn, and I walk back up those stairs.

CHAPTER 14

No one bothers me for the rest of the night, other than a worker who knocks, leaving a dinner tray.

I take a few nibbles, but my stomach is in too many knots to eat.

So, I take a shower, washing the blood sprays from my skin and hair. I crawl into bed, too tired to even dress, and fall fast asleep.

A baby cries.

Over and over.

Howling, rushing wind blows all around, unrelenting with its strength. It's cold. So bitterly, deathly cold.

"Here," a gentle voice says, and something that smells like animal, but is warm, wraps around my shoulders.

The baby cries again, wailing. Inconsolable.

"He'll die if we don't do something," the words breathe over my lips. The baby screams again, and tears prick in my eyes.

"There," the voice says. A hand raises, pointing across the valley. To the other side of the lake. Dark spires rise into the night air. "We will go there."

~

MY EYES SLIDE OPEN, MY TEETH CHATTERING. I PULL THE blanket tighter around me to fight off the cold.

Only my room is plenty warm. There's no wind. No first signs of snow.

I've always had strange dreams. Imagined things I can't really explain. Images of landscapes I've never visited. Flashes of faces I've never seen before. Had feelings of family and friends I know don't exist.

It's why I firmly believe in reincarnation.

I've lived other lives. It sounds crazy. But I can't come up with any other explanation.

My imagination isn't vivid enough to come up with this on its own.

The door to my bedroom opens and Mina walks in, pushing another meal cart.

"The King wants you to eat a good breakfast and enjoy the services he will soon be sending up," she says without hesitating or even looking up at me. She parks the meal cart close to my bed. I scramble, sitting up, but being careful to keep myself covered, considering I slept in the nude last night.

"The party will begin at two o'clock," Mina continues. She moves to my closet. She grabs another garment bag, this one huge. "You'll wear this. Head to the great hall, and he will meet you there."

She turns on her heel, and exits the bedroom.

I shake my head.

My life is so weird now.

I wrap a sheet around myself and sit on the edge of the bed, pulling the silver dome off the plate.

It's a large spread, far more than I could ever actually finish. Eggs, fruit, French toast, bacon. I can't think of any breakfast item that isn't there.

Almost as if on cue, as soon as I finish my breakfast, there's a knock on the door, but before I can even get up to answer, it opens and in walks a strong-looking man, carrying a massage table.

"Good morning, Miss Pierce," he greets me with a warm smile.

So much for any semblance of control over my life, or privacy.

I can't complain too much though, when ten minutes later a little groan of pleasure embarrassingly escapes my lips as the man digs his hands into my muscles. Expertly, he rubs, soothing, relaxing.

I really should thank Cyrus. It was a thoughtful move.

I get the impression he wants something from me. And as I think about it, I know exactly what it is.

He wants me to agree to let him kill me early.

My skin tingles as I think back to what happened last night. When he was brushing his skin against mine. The heady look in his eyes.

I can't lie. That was desire pulsing through my own veins.

But what is it that Cyrus really wants from me? Cyrus says and gets what he wants, so if he wanted me, for whatever primal or romantic purposes, I think he would just say it. And he had this urgency from the first sixty seconds of our meeting.

Desire might be evolving from it, but that's not what this stemmed from.

An hour later, the masseuse leaves and I shower, rinsing all the oils from my body and hair. When I step out of the bathroom, I'm glad I wear a robe, because two women wait for me. One wielding a rolling bag of hair stuff, another filled with cosmetics.

Nervously, I watch the clock tick closer and closer toward two o'clock. These women obviously know what they're doing. The one styles my hair into a sweeping, elegant up do, with loose curls and strands framing my face. She places a golden laurel branch into one side of it.

The other expertly applies my make-up. Dark and golden and fierce. But surprisingly, she doesn't use mass amounts of it. Just enough to highlight my natural features, and enough to make me look the part of someone strong enough to stand as a human in a room full of vampires.

They finish at a quarter to two, and offer to help me into my dress.

Nervous, I zip the garment bag open, scared to see Cyrus newest pick for my wear.

Gold.

So much gold.

The women *oo* and *ah* over the dress as carefully, so carefully, they help me into it.

It's a mermaid style, hugging my hips and the skirt fans out just above my knees, spilling in soft, golden silk to the floor.

The upper half hugs my hips, my waist, my chest. A halter top circles my neck before splitting down the middle, exposing the space between my breasts, dipping down to nearly my bellybutton before closing up again. It is adorned entirely with golden feathers. Soft, shimmering.

I step in front of a mirror, and even *my* breath is taken away.

I look like...like a goddess. The goddess of phoenixes, wife of Midas. Ready to blind the world, or burn it to the ground.

"It's..." I breathe. "Incredible."

But when I turn to thank my helpers, they're already gone.

My heart leaps into my throat when I look at the clock and find it five minutes to the hour. I slip my feet into the matching gold sandals and walk out of the suite.

My heart pounds, faster and faster as I rise, headed back up to the top floor.

And I realize, it's because of Cyrus.

I keep picturing his reaction to seeing me.

Suddenly the doors slide open.

It's a black and gold wonderland. The lights overhead reflecting off the mirrors have changed from blue and purple to gold. Everyone who mills about wears black, but gold masks adorn their faces.

Across the room, my eyes immediately search for him, and there he is. Sitting upon his throne, wearing that crown.

Cyrus' eyes lock with mine.

He rises.

And slowly smiles.

The rest of the room seems to sense a shift. The space grows quieter. And slowly I feel eyes turn in our direction.

I take a step forward. My heart races.

Cyrus also steps forward.

It takes an eternity to cross the great hall. The pressure of so many eyes watching is intense, intimidating. But I meet Cyrus' eyes. And like locking in, I'm drawn toward him, one step at a time.

Finally, we meet in the middle.

Cyrus extends a hand, and I place mine in his. He takes a deep bow, reverently pressing a kiss to my knuckles.

"Ravishing doesn't quite describe the way you look, Logan," he says as he looks up at me from beneath his eyelashes.

Thump, thump, thump my heart crashes against my ribcage.

Suddenly, the sound of a string quartet fills the space, one long, drawn out note, rising to a cliff, approaching the drop off.

Cyrus wraps his other hand around my waist and I draw in a quick breath at his nearness. He clasps my other hand, holding it up and out.

And with that mischievous, dubious smile, he leads me into the dance.

I am not a clumsy person. But I've certainly never been a dancer. Yet, with Cyrus leading me, we elegantly glide over the black marble floor, one sweeping step at a time.

"Does it feel real yet?" Cyrus whispers. "This life that awaits you?"

Everything from this weekend flashes through my mind. The wealth. The fangs. The blood. The brutality and strength.

"I think I understand now," I say. I can't look away from his eyes. "It's real. I still just don't know what my place will be in it once this time is up."

"That will become more clear once you Resurrect," he says. His grip on me tightens just slightly. "I promise, you will find your place, Logan Pierce."

"And what if I am not what you hope when I wake up?" I say. A painful monster takes up residence in my chest at the implications. "Will you just walk away then? Once you have your answer, then am I just on my own and you're done with me?"

He doesn't immediately respond. He studies me, my face. My hair. His eyes drop to the space between us. His eyes slide closed and I hear him take in a deep breath. We slowly turn and he pulls me just slightly closer before looking back up and meeting my eyes.

"Will you not be so very eager for me to walk away and leave you to yourself?" he finally asks.

And my feet still for a moment.

I stare into Cyrus' eyes.

He literally walked into my life with the intent to kill me. I've watched him do terrible, dangerous things. I've witnessed his temper and his wicked delight at the pain of others.

But I've seen that pain. I've witnessed that vulnerability and loneliness.

What I said to Amelia is true. He can take my acid. My bitterness.

"I think now that my eyes are open, it will be difficult to go back," is all that I can answer with honestly.

He pauses for a beat. But then he pulls me closer, and leads me into the dance once more.

The song ends, leading into another, and now the House of Valdez joins in. It's old. Choreographed. But by watching the others, by following Cyrus' lead, I go through the motions and steps without looking like a fool.

When it ends, Cyrus takes my hand and leads me toward the throne. I sit in the one beside him, turning my eyes out toward the crowd.

"Why didn't you tell me who you were right away?" I ask, watching Edmond dancing with a young woman with brilliant red hair. He twirls her and pulls her in close, smiling down at her.

"We made a unique bargain," Cyrus says. He watches the crowd as well. "That I had to get to know you. I did not believe you would behave as genuinely if you knew just who I was."

I shake my head. "I still don't, really. You, being King. I think I have a few questions."

He looks over, his eyes fixing on my lips. "Ask them, and I will do my best to answer them."

Nothing ever is a straight answer in the world of vampires.

"Are you King over all of them?" I ask. "You told me there are…twenty-seven Houses around the world. The Royal and the Born. Are you King over them all?"

"Yes," he says, still staring at my lips.

"That's the entire world," I breathe. "How have you commanded *all* their respect?"

His eyes rise up to mine and it sets my skin on fire. "Because I created them all."

The words steal my breath. They're too big. "What does that mean?"

Cyrus looks away, observing the vampires before him, the Born and the Royal. "I told you I am old. So old I have no idea how many millennia or centuries have passed anymore."

Tingles work their way up my arms, down the back of my neck, along my spine.

"I was always a curious man," Cyrus continues to explain. "A man who wanted to understand everything. To see what changes could be brought through science. And I knew I could never learn everything I desired in the short amount of days I would roam this earth."

I feel it. Time. Like a tangible thing Cyrus has invited as a special guest to this ball. It rolls in, overwhelming me.

"I became obsessed with my own immortality," he continues. "And so, I created the cure. With magic and science. I became what I am today."

Magic. Science.

"You made yourself immortal?" I question.

Cyrus nods. "I was strong. Keen. I felt infinite and unstoppable."

His hand curls into a fist. His jaw tightens and he watches as his knuckles turn white. "But I was cursed for my ambitious desires. I was no longer human. But now...I craved what pulsed through their veins. And my predator instincts, that science I had used, it made it so easy."

The image of him sinking his fangs into that woman's neck flashes before my eyes.

"I am the first vampire," Cyrus says. "The genesis of a new species."

It's incredible, really. If what he says is the truth. And every nerve in me, so aware and keen and on overload, says that it is.

"My wife," he says, and the words nearly choke in his throat. His eyes drop down, go hazy. "She was at my side this entire time, but when I ended the first human life by draining him of his blood, she was afraid of me."

This. *This* is the pain I see buried so deep in the man beside me.

"She wanted me to find a way to reverse it. But I couldn't." He shakes his head. "I didn't want to. I wanted her to join me. So that we could be together. Forever."

The agony is all over every inch of his stiff, barely controlled expression.

"In the end, I did not give her the option," he says. "I gave her the cure while she slept. And when she woke, she was as I was."

It makes me sick. To think how his poor wife must have felt when she realized.

"What I did not know," he says roughly. There's anger in his voice. Malice. "Was that she was pregnant before I turned her."

An actual gasp slips from my lips.

Cyrus' hand curls around the arm of the throne. He squeezes. It bends further.

"Months later, she gave birth to a son," he says. His voice is filled with bitterness and hatred. "And he was human. Absolutely human. We were trilled. So loving, so enthralled with this beautiful child. He grew and matured."

The bitterness in his voice grows thicker. "But that child was born with his own mind. He saw us, his parents, understood what we were capable of. He begged me to turn him on his thirteenth birthday and my wife and I refused."

No.

No. I don't like the turn this story is taking. Not one bit of it.

"He tried to convince us that we could use our abilities for so much more. That we could control the world if we wished. I saw the darkness in our son, but I refused to accept that we could not train it out of him. That we couldn't love him back from the darkness."

I feel it. That darkness.

"Soon after he turned eighteen, he died," Cyrus says. My heart cuts off, as abruptly as the change in the story. "A horrible, unforeseeable accident. I carried my son back to my wife. And even though we had struggled with him so much, even though we feared how his mind worked, we grieved him."

Cyrus' voice cracks slightly. I look up into his face. He stares down at his lap, his eyes unfocused. A mix of emotions holds him in their grasp: grief, anger, bitterness.

"But four days after we buried our son," Cyrus continues. "He rose from the grave. With glowing red eyes, strength like my own, he clawed his way through the ground and knocked down the doors to our home."

Ill. I feel ill. Shivers work their way down my spine.

"And from there, we lost all control," Cyrus says. "He went his own way, the first Born vampire. Human at birth, rising from his first death as a vampire."

Cyrus raises his head now, staring out over the dancing crowd. I look out at them as well.

They have to know this story. It's a part of their history.

"Years passed, and I knew I must prepare. I bought loyalty and armies over centuries. Because word had been spreading that my son had managed to conceive his own children, with human women, who then died and just like him, rose from the grave. He was creating his own army of immortal heirs."

I think of the span of time this must have taken place. First, Cyrus' son had to grow to an eighteen-year-old man. And then go off on his own. Impregnate women. Wait for them to be born and somehow discover that they could Resurrect just like himself.

Centuries, Cyrus had said.

"We both grew in power," Cyrus says. "With armies and loyal followers. A division formed, those who wanted to take over the world with my son. And those who knew we had to keep in secret if we did not wish to be eliminated. And eventually, it came to war."

How many centuries ago was this? How was it kept in the shadows, so secret? How is this not known to the world?

"My son conceived seven sons, all capable of producing their own immortal Born," Cyrus says. "He had twelve daughters, as well. In the end, two of his sons turned against him, allying with me, and three of his daughters. The rest stood with their father."

"You won the war," I breathe, my first words in what feels like centuries.

Cyrus nods. "It was not short. It was not clean. But in the end, I cleaved my own son's head from his shoulders, and declared the battle finished."

My blood stops in my body, absolutely cold.

"I banished or killed my five grandsons who turned against me. But they went about the world, producing more and more offspring. They were cut off from the family. From power, for after that time, I declared myself King, so nothing like this could ever happen again."

He looks down at his hand, and I see scars there.

"Those early years were not easy. Bloody, cold wars continued as we sorted through political systems and rules. But you see us now, today." He looks up, lifting his chin slightly. "We are organized. We operate under a smooth system. The descendants of the Royals rule the Houses, keeping the Born in check. Keeping sure our kind stay hidden."

I can hardly breathe. It's all so much. So big.

So incredible. So tragic.

But also beautiful.

"What about your wife?" I ask. He stiffens, but doesn't look toward me. "You said you made her like yourself. What happened to her?"

He pauses. And I can't pinpoint his reaction. "She died," he says simply.

And suddenly he rises from his throne. He steps forward into the crowd. He extends a hand to a woman, bowing, and then he pulls her into a dance.

It's whiplash. The tale cut too short, too quick. I need a better resolution than the one he just gave.

Slowly, Edmond walks over, pinning me with his dark eyes. He stops just in front of me, and holds out a hand.

"There might not have been only one victor in the end," he says. "But I will still take that prize and ask for a dance."

I look at him warily. He certainly didn't look too pleased with me after I stopped the dance, and then again during the gladiator fights. I'm not sure if I can trust him right now.

But I'm no coward.

I take his hand and follow him out onto the floor. He places a hand on my back and leads me into the steps.

"I don't think I understand you, Logan," he says. "You're hard. There's a bitterness in your eyes. You possess your own brand of cruelty and little tolerance." He twirls me under his arm before pulling me back. "But I know the reasons you've done it. And they're surprisingly tender, considering they are for a man whose cruelty and demands know no equal."

"I don't think it matters that you don't understand me," I say as he dips me. "I'll be leaving soon and you'll likely never see me again."

"Oh, I very much doubt that," he says as he lifts me once more. "There's certainly something special about you. If there weren't, the King wouldn't be looking at you like that."

And my eyes suddenly flick up, searching the room.

I instantly find him. Cyrus watches me over the shoulder of the woman he dances with. He's intense. Focused. His lips are sealed shut tightly.

"You all know what he wants from me, don't you?" I say as Edmond twirls me away, and my view of Cyrus is broken.

"The entire world of vampires, Born and Royal alike, know what he wants," he says. "But we also understand that it is not our place to tell the tale."

The music crescendos. His hands go to my waist and he lifts me. I rise through the air, feeling utterly weightless in his strong hands.

His eyes dare me to ask. To demand that he tells me what it is they're all waiting to see in me.

So, I won't.

I can be a petulant little beast when I want.

"A few weeks ago, at my work," I say, changing the subject, "there was a woman who had been ripped apart. And then another had been killed soon after her. The man I watched you kill in that alley. He was a vampire. He was the one who killed them, wasn't he?"

Edmond smiles and guides me through the steps. "Yes. He was an associate of our House years back. He was always a little…violent. But after he parted ways with us, his tendencies grew more sinister. We'd been tracking him for four weeks when we finally caught up with him in your town."

I shiver. How many deaths are written off as animal attacks, or the work of some insidious human, when really, it was vampires?

And I'm destined to be one of them soon.

"So, if you're not who the King hopes you are, do you think you'll go meet your mother?" Edmond asks.

Like he smacked me across the face, I stagger back just a step. I look up at him with surprised eyes.

"You might as well," he says. He's enjoying knocking me on my ass. I can see it in his eyes. "The second we release Rath, he'll go running back to Alivia and tell her everything that's happened. If you don't go to her, she'll come looking for you."

My throat is tight. My brows furrow. But I can't find an answer to his question.

"It's something you should know about the House of Conrath," Edmond says. "We're a family here in the House of Valdez. But not like they are."

"Cyrus said she manipulated them all into being a part of her House," I say through a tight throat.

Edmond shakes his head. "It might have started out that way. But not anymore. I meant that they're *family*. The loyalty in that House." He shakes his head again. "I've never seen anything quite like it. They've died for each other. They'd do it again. All of them."

His statements take me aback.

Maybe…maybe there are two sides to the story. Cyrus is so bitter, so cold when he talks about my birth mother. But if someone like Edmond can say these things… Maybe she isn't everything I feared.

"Life is hard for any vampire living on their own," Edmond says as the music begins to wind down. "As a Royal, you're entitled to privilege. You're a rightful heir of that House. To more than one, possibly, if we can figure out who your father is. Or perhaps even Court."

My brows furrow. There's another one of those words everyone keeps saying, but I don't know the meaning of.

Edmond sighs and shakes his head. "You really don't know anything, do you?"

My eyes turn cold and I glare at him.

He smiles. "King Cyrus lives in his castle in Austria. *Roter Himmel*, it's called. But he's not alone. There are hundreds of Royal Born who live there, at Court. His favorites, or those who were born there. As my father said, my brother Horatio, has lived there for some time. He actually spent some time with your mother there. If your father is a member of the Court, you rightfully would have a place there."

I consider it, but an ache pulls in my chest.

If I'm not what Cyrus is searching for, I don't think I want to have to go there, seeing him, but knowing he wasn't interested in ever talking to me again.

"Consider your mother," Edmond says again, raising his eyebrows just slightly. The music ends, and with a knowing smile, he walks away.

I hear footsteps coming up from behind, and turn to see Cyrus approaching.

"It is time," he says. "I must return you to your home so that you may continue with our bargain."

I give a little nod, at a loss for any words.

"I thank you, House of Valdez," Cyrus says. He does not speak overly loud, but every head turns at his commanding voice. "Thank you for your impressive accommodations. Thank you for your hospitality. And thank you for providing such quality entertainment."

He holds out his hand, I take it, and without another word from the crowd, or from their King, he leads me back to the elevator.

He's tight. That's the best way I can describe it as we silently ride the elevator down. He's wrapped up in his own thoughts, lost in possibly thousands of years of memories.

So, I let him be.

We exit onto our floor and silently we both part ways into

our rooms to change. I pull on another pair of shorts and a shirt. As soon as I'm done, Mina packs up my dress, and places it with my other bags, which have already been packed.

When we walk into the common room, I find Cyrus and Fredrick, waiting. He still does not say anything as we take the elevator back to the ground floor and then climb into a limo, which drives us to the airport.

It's dark by the time we climb aboard Cyrus' jet. Ten o'clock. The lights are dim as I sit in my same seat as before, and Cyrus takes his place, as well. Fredrick and Mina sit toward the back, but this time they just relax into their seats in silence. No more frantic planning.

We take off into the night sky.

Just twenty minutes before we land in Denver, Cyrus says, "Was Las Vegas what you expected?"

I look up at him. He's looking back at me. But his expression is different. It's distant. He's still lost in his own head.

"No," I say, looking out the window. "It was so much… more. It was everything you wanted it to be for me, though. It had the desired effect. But…"

"What?" he encourages when I hesitate.

I take a breath. "I think I enjoyed it." I blush at the confession. "Not every second of it. But…there were parts that I think I enjoyed."

He blinks. Three times.

He reaches forward, taking my hand.

And we both look back out at the night sky as we land in Colorado.

CHAPTER 15

JUST A FRIENDLY LITTLE REMINDER, THE TEXT READS, *$1,000, 3 more days.*

I swear under my breath as I pack up at work. With shaking fingers, I text back, *I know.* I step out into the blinding sun after work on Monday. Mentally, I think through all of my things again, considering what I could sell to come up with the extra five hundred.

Nothing. Nothing I own is worth that much money.

Short of selling my body for services, I can't think of anything I can do to come up with the money before Thursday.

"You seem tense," Mina says as we both slide into my car.

"Not all of us can afford to buy mansions at the drop of a hat," I say, annoyed. I pull out of the parking lot and head onto the road.

"If money is what has you so stressed out, perhaps you should talk to Cyrus," she says. "You are a Royal, after all. That entitles you to certain benefits."

My brows furrow and I look over at her in surprise.

Money.

Cyrus obviously has plenty of it. He's had thousands of years to earn it.

And the Houses. There has to be a source that supports them in some way.

Of course it's Cyrus.

"No," I say, shaking my head. "I can take care of myself."

It's obviously not true. But I can't stomach the idea of crawling to Cyrus and begging for his financial help.

Mina shrugs and doesn't say anything more.

I pull into the parking lot of my apartment. "I'll be right back, you can just wait here," I tell Mina.

With heavy feet, I trudge up the stairs.

Harvey, my slimy landlord waits for me at my old door, standing in it, an obvious sign of *not a chance you're getting back inside*, written all over his body language, his burly chest blocking my way.

Good thing Cyrus and I got everything last week.

He only scowls at me as I hand over the key.

I hand over my freedom. My thread of adulthood. My backup option.

I can't even look up at him as I turn to go.

My stomach sinks.

It's so final. I may not have had another choice in giving

up my apartment. But this feels like the first item crossed off the list in saying goodbye to my human life.

Silently, I climb in the car, and we drive back to Cyrus' house. Back home.

We walk through the grand doors. And I'm just too heavy. Too tired. Too everything.

I barely even glance up at Cyrus as I walk in. His head perks up, but maybe he knows how to read me, now. He doesn't say anything.

I head up to my room. I curl up in the bed. And I just try not to think.

Two more days, Shylock texts me on Tuesday.

One more day, he sends on Wednesday.

I'm sweating bullets. I don't sleep. Anxiety crawls its way up my chest all day at work.

I consider asking Emmanuel if I can borrow it. But then I'm just in debt to one more source, and then I'd be dragging him into my mess.

When I get home, I find myself scanning the house.

Anything. I could take anything from here, sell it, and have enough money.

But that only makes me a thief.

All I can do is show up at the meeting place tomorrow and beg for more time. And mercy.

"I have a thing I have to take care of tonight," I say on Thursday morning. "I'll only be gone for about thirty minutes. I haven't tried to run yet, and I don't plan on doing it now. So Mina can take the evening off."

I say it all in a rush while staring into the fridge. I'm not hungry. My stomach is full of knots. There's not a chance I can eat. But it's habit, and there's something human and comforting about habit.

"From your tone I assume you're not going to say what this 'thing' is," Cyrus states.

He's just walked down the stairs and stands in the doorway to the living area. His hair is wet, slicked back. He slowly buttons up his shirt. He leaves the top three open.

"It's all part of our deal," I say emptily. "Closing up my human life."

Cyrus looks up at Mina, who gives him a doubtful look.

"You can take the night off, Mina," Cyrus says as he begins rolling up his cuffs, exposing his lean forearms. "I trust Logan when she says she won't run."

I nod my head in thanks as I close the fridge. I grab my purse off the counter and head for the door.

I feel Cyrus' eyes on me as I walk past him, but I don't have the mental energy to put on a show of strength and bravado for him.

It's the longest and fastest day of work, ever.

I keep looking at the clock every five minutes. Every time I look, it's half an hour later.

Time speeds along, and all too soon, it's five and I'm clocking out. Mina and I drive back to the house.

Fredrick is serving dinner, and no one says a word as we eat.

At twenty to seven, I head to my bedroom. I pull open my bottom drawer and pull the folded up hundred dollar bills from a sock. Only five of them. Not enough. But it's everything I have.

I suppose it's a good thing vampires still have to eat. I wouldn't be able to afford to feed myself if I wasn't living here in this house.

I may not have had a choice, but there have been several unexpected benefits to being a prisoner.

"I'll be back soon," I say when I reach the bottom of the stairs. I don't even look around to see if anyone is around to hear me.

I imagine all the bones Shylock could break as I drive to our meeting place. Fingers. Toes. Legs, if he's feeling particularly angry over five hundred dollars. Maybe my nose. A black eye might satisfy him over a few weeks' delay.

By the time I pull into the parking lot of the gas station, I'm about ready to puke. Every one of my nerves is on high alert. Fight or flight is raging through my system at supersonic speed.

I'd run.

Without a doubt.

But he knows where to find the people I care about.

My knees quake as I climb out of my car. Half of me feels numb as I walk around to the back of the building, to the narrow alley between the shops behind it.

He's already waiting.

The moment I step into the alley, he pushes off the wall and walks toward me.

Shylock. The money shark. The man I turned to when everything in my life fell apart.

The shark that's been breathing down my neck for the past two years.

"Let's make this quick," he says, looking around to be sure no one is watching. "I have another appointment after this."

Appointment—as in someone else to scare half to death.

Shylock is tall. Probably weighs two hundred fifty pounds. His too-thin hair hangs long and dirty down his back. He wears a long black jacket, even though it's summer. Black boots are strapped around his ankles.

Picture a money-loaning lowlife, and you can imagine Shylock.

"I…" I stutter, and I hate it. I need to sell this. "I need another week. I have half now, but you moving up the date like this-"

"Excuse me?" he says, leaning in, his face too close. "I said today. You agreed to my terms, however flexible they may need to be, back when you came to me. Twice." He growls, his breath fowl. I barely hold back a gag. "I said today. Payment will be made today."

I swallow once. I reach into my pocket with trembling hands. "I have five hundred now," I say, forcing my voice not to quiver. "I'll have the rest a week from today."

Shylock snatches the money from my hand and I flinch back half a step.

His hand lurches out, grabbing the front of my shirt. He

yanks me forward into his face as he slips the money into his pocket.

"Not good enough, *Lo*," he hisses, using Amelia's nickname for me. "And now I'm going to have to charge you some kind of interest."

He pulls me closer, crushing us chest to chest. I let out a little squeal, a mix of anger and fear. He reaches forward, sliding his hand down my backside.

I shove against him, but he yanks me close again. The fabric of my shirt rips at the collar, tearing halfway down to my stomach.

I let out an angry cry, shoving against him again, but he just gives a disgusting little laugh and pulls me forward with his hands cupped around my rear.

"She's a feisty little fighter," he breathes, pressing his nose into my ear, whispering against my cheek.

"Get your slimy hands off of me," I growl, shoving against the man who outweighs me by well over a hundred pounds.

He just laughs again. With his weight, he backs me against the wall, and I smash into it, pain shooting out along the contact points. He reaches down between us, searching for the button of my pants.

A low growl whips both of our heads to the left.

Through the dim light, a pair of glowing red eyes stares us down.

"I was going to intervene," a low, calm but dangerous voice says. And my pulse skyrockets. "I was going to offer to pay her debt off and let you go your own way." One step,

Cyrus enters the alleyway. "But then you had to go and put your hands on her. And touching my things is an unforgiveable sin."

Shylock is stiff, wary.

Cyrus is smaller than Shylock. Shorter. Not as muscled.

But when a man with glowing red eyes is fixated on you, when he speaks with dangerous, controlled words, you'd best fear for your life.

"This here has nothing to do with you, freak," Shylock growls. But there's a hint of uncertainty in his voice. "Just keep walking."

Cyrus smiles, and oh how terrifying the man's smile is.

"Oh, but it has a great deal to do with me," he says. "You've threatened this rather incredible woman. And now you've put her hands on her."

Shylock spits in Cyrus' direction, landing on his boot.

And like he can really ignore Cyrus' presence, Shylock searches again, and this time succeeds in unbuttoning my pants.

One second he was there. The next, Shylock is gone.

A scream is strangled from my throat when I'm nearly knocked over as Cyrus pounces on Shylock. They hit the ground ten feet from me, rolling only once.

Cyrus lands on top of him. One hand wraps around Shylock's throat. He looks up at the King with wide, terrified eyes.

Cyrus leans in close, their noses only two inches apart.

"Perhaps the world has forgotten common decency," Cyrus says in that controlled voice of his. "This world is full of all kinds of predators. I would know since I made the most powerful ones. But you..." he trails off, his lip curling in a sneer. "You are the worst kind."

I can't figure out what happened at first.

There's a little pop sound.

Shylocks eyes go wide.

They stay that way.

Even when his head relaxes back a bit.

And then there's blood.

One short breath huffs out of my mouth. And then I press my hands over it, trapping the scream behind them.

Cyrus squeezed.

And squeezed.

And squeezed right through his neck. Snapping his head right off.

I turn, crouching down into a squat, holding my hands over my mouth so that the screams don't spill from my lips.

Sharp breaths pull in and out of my nose and tears prick my eyes.

I'm not sure how much time passes. I hear the sound of the dumpster at the end of the alley open and close, something heavy hits the metal bottom.

But then there's a warm hand on my back.

And the emotions rip through me at tornado speed.

I shakily rise to my feet.

And I bury my face in Cyrus' chest, letting tears overtake me.

He wraps his arms around my back, holding me close. "It's over," he whispers. "He'll never, ever bother you again.

Whatever debt you owed him, you'll never have to worry about it again."

I sob. I tremble.

Because all I can think about is the feeling of Shylock's hands on my rear. His fingers slipping inside my waistband to unbutton my pants. The evil look in his eyes as he decided exactly what kind of interest I would pay.

"It's over," Cyrus whispers again, pulling me closer.

Shylock would have raped me.

His fingers were right there.

Too strong, too possessive. The look in his eyes told me everything.

He would have taken me, right here in this alley.

"Let's go home," Cyrus says quietly, cradling my head against his chest.

I squeeze him tighter, clinging to him.

Safe.

Not just safe, *protected.*

And those two words, they make me pull back, and I look up into Cyrus' eyes. They no longer glow red. He looks back at me, and everything in his eyes echoes those two words.

How? I think to myself. *How could I possibly feel that way around this dangerous man?*

"Come on," Cyrus says. He takes a step back, but takes my hand, guiding me. To my car, he leads me. He opens the passenger door and I sink into it. As I give him the keys, I realize my shirt is torn open, exposing my chest and most of my stomach. I pull the fabric closed, attempting to cover myself.

With slightly jerky movements, Cyrus drives us back to the mansion.

I'm numb. Not in the present. I don't even remember walking up the stairs, but suddenly I hear the sound of a door shutting and look around to realize I'm in my room. Cyrus stands at the door, looking at me with concerned eyes.

"Thank you," I whisper. And he holds me there, captive.

"I apologize," he says. He takes one step closer, but no more. "I should have intervened sooner. I-"

I shake my head. "You stopped a very bad man from doing something very…" my voice cracks just a bit. "Very bad. Thank you."

Cyrus' lips form a thin line. I see all kinds of questions in his eyes. He gives a small nod.

I walk to my closet. I'm so out of it, I forget to even close the door as I change.

I throw the clothes in the trash. I don't ever want to see them again, remember the feel of his hand on the outside of them, see the button he undid.

I put on a pair of sweats and pull on a tank top.

Cyrus sits in the chair in the corner when I walk out. I sink onto the bed and stare at the floor.

"I went to Shylock for the money to finish school," I explain without him even asking. "I told you that I had enough money to finish one semester after my money was stolen from my car. The bank wouldn't loan me anything. My parents didn't have enough. So I asked around, and Shylock's name came up."

I shake my head, thinking how stupid, *stupid* I had been

to go to someone like him. I should have just taken a few semesters off, worked. But I'd been so determined to keep going.

"He loaned me all the money up front. Set up a payment schedule." My throat is thick. "It was ambitious; I knew I'd barely be able to keep up with it. But I was desperate, so I agreed. I was keeping up with it by working nights while I was at school. I didn't get more than a few hours of sleep here and there, but I was making it work."

I nod, thinking of those ever-tired days. I was always exhausted. Falling asleep in classes at times. Occasionally falling asleep at work. But somehow I always got away with it.

"But then in January my dad had an accident," I say, remembering when my mom had called me. "He'd fallen off a roof he'd been working on. He broke his back."

My chest hurts. I grip the neck of my top, clinging to that ache.

"He wasn't paralyzed, but he needed surgery, and he was going to have to learn how to walk again." I picture my dad, getting rolled away to the operating room. "He's self-employed, so insurance is always a nightmare. He didn't realize his insurance hadn't renewed. So suddenly they were slammed with tens of thousands of dollars in bills. They...they were going to lose their house, 'cause Dad couldn't work. Mom about had a heart attack from the stress."

I squeeze my eyes closed, remembering sitting with Mom at the kitchen counter while she just sobbed. Eshan sat on the other side of her, trying to keep it together, but he didn't know what to do either.

"I borrowed another ten thousand from Shylock and paid their mortgage without them knowing," I continue. "They thought some of the neighbors had helped out. But when I borrowed more, the payments went up and Shylock got a lot more demanding. I started at the mortuary and was making more money, and things were okay for a few months. But then Amelia moved in with her boyfriend and I had all of the rent to cover by myself. And I just..." I suck in a breath. "I couldn't keep up."

"This is what's been bothering you all week," Cyrus says, leaning forward, fixing his eyes on me. "That lowlife has been holding this over your head."

I nod with my eyes fixed on the ground.

I hear Cyrus stand and he sits on the bed beside me.

"I know you're fiercely independent, Logan," he says. He sits near, but he does not touch me. "You're determined to take care of yourself, and everything you've done to do so, and help your family, it's commendable." He shifts, taking something out of his pocket. He holds out a piece of paper. It has an account number on it, and a card taped to it. "Fredrick got this set up just after we confirmed you are a Royal. You will never have to worry about money again, as a Royal. Of course, it is up to you if you ever wish to use it or not."

Tears pool in my eyes as I take the paper. My lip trembles.

I'm strong. I'm nasty when I want to be. I can sling hurtful words and show anyone who's boss.

But right now, I'm just a girl who was nearly assaulted.

I'm just a girl who is so thankful to the man beside her, but so confused all at the same time.

So for just this moment I let a little bit of vulnerability show. I lean into Cyrus, and let him cradle me against his chest and hold me as I shake.

CHAPTER 16

The weight off my shoulders is an incredible thing.

As I get ready for work the next day, I physically feel lighter. I feel like smiling. I feel like going for a walk in the sun. I feel like visiting my family and actually laughing with them.

I walk down the stairs Friday morning. Cyrus stands at the counter talking to Fredrick in German, their words rough, hurried, with urgency.

He looks over and catches my eye.

I feel myself actually blush, a smile blooms on my face.

And one slowly grows on his face.

My heart skips a beat and a butterfly does an elaborate backflip in my stomach.

Oh, this is so complicated.

"Did you sleep well?" Cyrus asks, turning and leaning against the counter.

I tuck a lock of hair behind my ear, pulling a chair out at the dining table. "I did. Thanks."

Fredrick scurries over and sets a plate down on the table. Scrambled eggs, sliced fruit, and toast.

I glance up once more as I sit, and find Cyrus watching me with that little smile.

I sit and even though my stomach is busy acting like a fourteen-year-old girl, I take small bites.

My phone dings with a text and I pull it out of my back pocket.

Amelia called. She told me you have a boyfriend?! And that it's getting super serious!! Why haven't you told me?? When can I meet him?!?!

Mom.

I feel my face flush and I glance up at Cyrus once, but he's turned back to Fredrick, picking at his own breakfast.

It's still really new, I respond. *We're just kind of figuring things out. I don't know if meeting him now is the time.*

Don't try to pull that on me, Mom responds. *Amelia said you've gone and moved in with him! If it's serious enough to be living together already, it's serious enough for us to meet him!*

I groan, and immediately realize my mistake. Cyrus looks over.

"What's wrong?" he asks, and there's glowing embers in his eyes, ready to tear down the world.

I sigh and shake my head. "Nothing. Just...real world drama. It's a little difficult to explain what's been going on to certain people."

194

Cyrus studies me, as if he can lift the full truth off of my face.

I'll think about it, I text Mom back.

She texts back with a frowning face.

My good mood from this morning was first thrown by Mom's prying into what really isn't the truth, and then further when I get to work.

Emmanuel and I go to a home to pick up a body. That of a twenty-one-year-old girl who just lost her battle with cancer. The poor parents must have known it was coming. When we arrive they're just quiet and numb-looking. No tears. No wails of despair. Just emptiness in their eyes as we load their daughter and take her body away to prepare for burial.

My stomach feels hollow as I prepare her body.

She's so young. Only a year older than myself.

Her short hair is dyed a brilliant mermaid red. Her skin isn't wrinkled. The only mars to her body are from treatments.

Sometimes life isn't fair. Her life was cut too short. She wasn't given the opportunities she deserved.

When I walk out of work at five, I feel heavy. Tired.

So when I pull out my phone as I sit in my car, I actually appreciate the first text I see there.

I thought you should continue to enjoy your day. I told Mina her services were no longer required.

Cyrus.

I look up and around, and realize that Mina is, in fact, nowhere to be seen.

Cyrus is no longer requiring her to follow me at all times.

With a smile, one I really needed this evening, I open the other messages.

Amelia.

You promised me a double with you and your new man. I'm calling it in today. No excuses. It's Friday!

Another one from some point during the day: *I know you must have your hands buried in a dead person, but you better not bag out on me! I mean it, the four of us!*

And the last message, from thirty minutes ago: *Meet us at Lanes, seven o'clock, or I will disown you!*

I look at the time. If we're going to make it, I need to hurry. I still need to shower and change.

Fine! I quickly text her back. *We'll be there.*

I text Cyrus next. *We're going out tonight. Don't forget, your name is Collin, and we're madly in love…*

A moment later, the message shows as read, but he doesn't respond.

Whatever.

I toss my phone into the passenger seat and put the car into drive.

When I get home, it's quiet. I walk upstairs and hear the sound of the shower shutting off in the room Cyrus has claimed. With a smile, I head into my own room and go straight for the shower.

I dry my hair and style it into loose curls. My hair is long now, hanging most of the way down my back. I put on olive green shorts, and a white top that flatters my figure. Casual but cute. I top it off with a gold necklace and white sneakers.

I double check my reflection in the mirror, and smile.

A girl just needs to feel cute every once in a while.

Especially when her date, even if it's fake, is with a true blue king.

For a moment, the thought overwhelms me.

I'm a little in awe of myself. Of my audacity.

I've bossed the King around. Spat nasty words in his direction. For part of that I didn't really know who he was. But once I learned his true identity, I didn't exactly stop…

I know I'm not going to change. I'll still act the same. And I'm still going to smile. Because he takes my acid.

At six-thirty I step out of my room. Gently, I knock on Cyrus' door, but there's no response.

So, down the stairs I head, getting worried. It's too silly. I can't expect a man like Cyrus to play along. He's powerful and worldwide, and I'm just a twenty-year-old, insignificant girl.

But, as I descend the stairs, I see him standing there. He's wearing a pair of well-fitting jeans and a white V-neck t-shirt that highlights his very nice features. And he holds a bouquet of vibrantly blue flowers. Small, trumpet-shaped. Absolutely beautiful.

"I believe it has at times been customary to bring flowers to the woman you are madly in love with," Cyrus says with a mischievous smile as I step onto level ground.

I smile, stopping just before Cyrus and accepting the bouquet. "They're…" I give a little laugh, feeling silly that I'm blushing. "They're absolutely beautiful. What kind of flower are they?"

"Gentiana," he says and I can feel him studying me. "They commonly grow at home in Austria. I thought maybe you would appreciate them."

I smile, my eyes rising to meet Cyrus'. "They're absolutely beautiful. You didn't have to do this." My eyes fall. "I know it isn't real."

I feel his finger under my chin, raising it so I have to look at him. "You deserve them, Logan. Don't deny me something I wanted to do."

My face blushes, but I offer him a smile. "We...we better get going. They'll be waiting for us."

Cyrus nods, extending a hand toward the door that leads to the garage.

Quickly, I place the flowers in a vase on the table, and head to the car.

"You think you can handle the traffic?" I tease Cyrus as he takes the keys to that fancy sports car.

"I believe so," he says, fixing me with that mirthful look in his eye.

Donning a pair of sunglasses, because the sun still sits atop the mountains, Cyrus starts the car, and smooth as butter, he backs it out of the garage. Putting it in drive, he peels out, flying down the driveway.

Maybe it's the up and down day I've had. Maybe it's because I feel...*good* tonight. Maybe it's the man and what I know about him who sits beside me. But I let out a squeal, loosening up.

A smile. A wide, real, relaxed smile spreads on Cyrus' own face.

I guide him through town, and without any jerks, without any accidents, he carefully drives. And just before seven, he parks in the lot. He darts out, only to nearly instantly appear outside my door, which he opens, and extends a hand to pull me to my feet.

"Madly in love, you said?" Cyrus says as he closes my door and locks the car. "Just how hard do you want me to sell this to your friend?"

I blush as he hesitates by the car. "Let's just say she was more than a little shocked to hear I was 'moving in' with you. I've never..." I hesitate, feeling embarrassed. "I've never had a serious relationship. Or any kind of relationship. So to her, this seems like a really, really big deal."

He studies me, and I squirm under his intense gaze. But I also feel...open. Exposed in a way that I think I actually like.

This man, he's doing something to me.

"Have you ever been in love, Logan?" he asks.

His very serious question snares me, startling my eyes to his.

I don't answer immediately.

Even though the answer is an easy one. Simple.

"I've never found a man who didn't find me too...salty," I answer honestly. "So, no."

He stares at me for another long moment, and I swear, he's looking for something inside of me. Searching.

"Let's sell this," Cyrus says.

He holds his hand out. I look down and my heart rate triples.

I slide my fingers through his, relishing the electricity that rips through my body at the contact.

Together, we walk through the front doors of the bowling alley.

It's loud and smells of greasy food and sweat inside. I search through the crowd, scanning for familiar blonde hair and mile-long legs.

"Lo!" Amelia waves, flashing a brilliant smile from one of the further lanes.

I wave, and Cyrus and I head to the counter to pay and get some shoes.

"Really?" he says, quietly. "The first date I've gone on in centuries, and you make me wear shoes worn by hundreds of other people?"

I chuckle, because I see the smile creeping onto his lips. "I know. It's disgusting. But even though you wouldn't guess it from looking at her, Amelia loves bowling. And her boyfriend is like, super good at it."

Cyrus gives a mirthful little grimace, but follows me with the shoes toward our lane.

"There's my girl!" Amelia squeals as we walk up, hand-in-hand for show. She throws her arms around me, squeezing hard. "I can't believe how much I've missed you and it's only been a week."

"I missed you, too," I laugh, hugging my best friend. "And don't blame me, you're the one who caused this separation."

"Actually, I think I'm the one to blame." Tanner pipes up from behind.

"Yeah, you are," I accuse.

Cyrus steps forward, extending a hand. "Hello, I'm Collin."

"Tanner," he says.

And it just radiates off of Cyrus. The power. The time. The other worldliness. Because Tanner's expression is unsure. Intimidated. But he shakes Cyrus' hand, flashing a hesitant smile.

"It's a pleasure to meet more of Logan's friends." Cyrus looks back at me, and wraps an arm over my shoulders, hugging me in tight.

Amelia squeals, her nose scrunching up as she smiles. "You two are just too damn cute, I just can't stand it! About time you got a man, Logan, so we can do fun things like this together!"

I blush, but look up at Cyrus.

And I could swear that was real admiration in his eyes as he looks down at me.

"Let's do this!" Tanner declares loudly. "Collin, I hope you're decent competition, because it's always a slaughter with these two."

"Oh," Cyrus muses. "I think I'll be able to keep up."

I SIT DOWN AFTER MY TURN, AFTER REALLY EMBARRASSING myself only knocking down two pins. Cyrus stands, reaching for my hand. He lifts it, gently pressing his lips to my knuckles. I feel myself blush—apparently I can't stop today—and he smiles as he steps up for his turn.

"Lo, this is incredible," Amelia says quietly as she watches Cyrus prepare to roll the ball down the lane. Tanner watches him from the side, his arms crossed over his chest, sweat breaking out on his forehead. Cyrus is certainly keeping up. "You two are amazing together. He's so…intense when he looks at you."

I smile, looking at Cyrus as he swings the ball. With perfect form, he sends it rolling down the lane.

"He's really something extraordinary," I say quietly. Though I didn't mean to say it out loud.

Amelia sighs. "This is going to be it for you, Lo. I can feel it. I can *see* it."

I laugh, looking over at my friend. "See it?"

Amelia nods. "You're glowing," she says with a dramatic whisper. Because Cyrus turns, his fists raised in triumph. He's just gotten another strike. He smiles, and I can't help but smile back.

"The way you look at him," Amelia says quietly, looking from Cyrus to me. "It's obvious how in love you already are."

My eyes snap to Amelia's, my brows narrowing. "What?" My throat is tight and the word comes out too high-pitched.

She rolls her eyes at me. "I know you're inexperienced, but come on, Lo. Can't you tell? You're completely and totally head-over-heels in love with Collin."

Her words send my heart into a tailspin.

Racing. Thundering. Skipping.

Frantically, I look toward Cyrus, with his enhanced hearing. But he's chatting happily with Tanner, who prepares for his turn.

"That's a *good* thing, in case you didn't realize," Amelia says, laying a hand on my leg. "You deserve to find someone who's the match to your incredible self."

It's kind of hard to breath. And I can't quite look at Cyrus again as he turns and comes to sit beside me now that his turn is over.

I hope and pray that he didn't hear what Amelia said, or how my internal organs reacted to her statement.

He reaches over and takes my hand once more, holding it protectively in his lap.

CHAPTER 17

LOGAN, THIS REALLY ISN'T COOL. MOM TEXTS ON MONDAY. *IF you're going to live with a guy this soon after meeting him, I at least need to see what all the fuss is about.*

Soon, I fend her off.

On Wednesday, she texts again. *Your father and I are going out tonight. Maybe you and Collin could join us?*

He has work, I lie.

I lie on my bed that night, unable to sleep, staring at the ceiling. Mom's been hounding me all day about this. And now that I'm finally alone, in the dark, I can sort through my own thoughts.

It's been subtle, but over the past few weeks as I've begun to see my reality, as Cyrus has shown me, I'm beginning to accept that this is going to be my world. The world of Royals, and Houses with power. Of blood and fangs. These are vampires. And I will be one of them soon.

The reason for them all is Cyrus. He created this world. Brought it into being. Ruled—rules it.

Can I really bring that man into my childhood home? Can I really introduce him to my family? My parents? My baby brother?

And can I really do that to them? Introduce them to that kind of man, and put on the show of the two of us being in love?

You're completely and totally head-over-heels in love with Collin.

Amelia's words echo through my head, over and over and over.

They can't be true.

Cyrus erupted into my life, only brought across the world because I look like my mother, who he so obviously despises. He sank his fangs into my flesh and then the look in his eyes changed.

Cyrus wants something from me.

Took control of my life to get it. Is still determined that I must die to get it.

So it's just not possible that I could be in love with him.

What kind of sick Stockholm Syndrome is that?

But I roll over onto my side, looking at the door.

I know he's in his bedroom. He went into it at the same time I came into mine. He walked across his bedroom floor, paced, for about an hour. But then I finally heard the rustle of his bed against the wall, the same one my own bed rests against.

I roll onto my knees and place my hands on the wall between us.

It's just not possible. Wouldn't make any sense. What does that make me if I developed feelings for a man like him?

I can't be in love with the King of vampires.

YOU NEED TO GIVE IN TO YOUR MOTHER, DAD TEXTS ME ON Friday night. *This is stressing her out and it's not fair. She has a right to want to meet her daughter's boyfriend.*

I sigh as I walk through the door on Friday after work.

I close it, leaning against it. I look up at the ceiling, feeling my stomach sink.

There are real world consequences for what is about to happen. For the path I'm being ushered down. My mother is going to think this is going somewhere it isn't.

This is the deal you made though, I think to myself. *You're supposed to be finishing your human life.*

And as I think about it, a cold drop of panic sinks into my stomach.

Today is the fourteenth. My death date is the twenty-forth.

I have ten days left to wrap up my human life.

With a gasp, I cross the entry and rush up the stairs. I shove open the door to my bedroom and head for the desk against the wall. Throwing open drawers, I sigh in relief when I find a notebook and a pen in another drawer.

Things to wrap up, I write in big bold letters across the top.

Work, I write on the first line. In less than ten days I'm going to have to quit. I realize now that I'm already too late to give two-weeks' notice. Emmanuel isn't going to be happy. He's always been so good to me. And now I'm going to leave him hanging.

Amelia, I scrawl on the next line.

Family, I write on the one after.

I need to tell them *something*.

Once I'm turned, if I don't just die for good, I doubt I can be around them for some time. I'm going to have to go away.

"Cyrus?" I call out before I even really think about it.

And almost as if he was just waiting for me, he's instantly there, standing in the doorway.

"If I really wake up after being dead for four days," I say, watching him, but not really seeing him. I'm imagining where I'll be while I'm dead. "What can I expect in those first few days?"

Cyrus leans against the doorway, watching me. "Your new body will be overwhelming in ways," he says. "The strength, the speed, the new sense of sight and hearing. But your body will already be perfectly adapted for it."

I nod, taking it in, but not really hearing him. "That's not what I'm talking about."

Cyrus' lips thin. But he nods. "You ask about the thirst."

I nod.

He takes a deep breath. He steps into the room, and slowly crosses the room to sit on my bed. "The thirst will be consuming when you first awaken. Your throat will burn with fire, your need for blood will be unquenchable. Only fresh blood will satisfy you."

"Meaning I will hurt someone," I say, swallowing once. I resist the instinct to raise a hand to my throat, which tingles.

"Yes," Cyrus whispers. "The first feeding is always a draining one. No matter how much you might not wish to hurt or kill someone, no one can stop themselves the first time."

Breathing is difficult, my throat is too tight.

I swear I can already taste the coppery wet of blood in the back of my throat.

"You'll need to feed often in the beginning, as your new body adjusts," Cyrus says.

"How long?" I ask. I clear my throat and blink. "You don't go running around, driven mad by bloodlust. Mina seems to have things under control. The House of Valdez wasn't attacking every human at the casino. How long until I have the thirst under control?"

He looks at me, again searching for something. "Everyone is different. For some they gain control in about three weeks. For others it's longer. A month, two. It's controllable if you're aware of your needs and take care of them. But most don't have full strength of will over the thirst until they've been Resurrected for a year or so."

A year.

A year before I won't pose a threat to my family. My friends.

"Where will I go?" I ask in a whisper. "I can't stay here. I will have to tell everyone something. Give them some reason why I won't see them for such a long time. But I do have to go somewhere."

Cyrus stands, and I can nearly see the weight upon his shoulders. "That will become very clear once the end of the month has arrived." He goes to stand in the doorway and looks back. "Logan, are you sure you still wish to wait so long? The uncertainty could be over in four days."

My chest aches. Splinters at the look in his eyes.

"I need to say goodbye," I say quietly. And I hate that I can't give him what he wants.

Cyrus only nods, and walks out of the room, as if it hurts too much to stay.

I look back down at my list.

I need to leave for a year.

Where I'm going, no one will say. My future is uncertain. But the lie is not.

And there, working on the list, on all the things I need to wrap up, I come up with the lie, with the plan, that I will tell everyone I care about.

CHAPTER 18

We're coming over on Sunday, I text my mom that night.

I tell Cyrus to get ready, tell him to play along with everything I say when we go over, and he agrees.

All the little pieces I plan out, crafting my lie so intricately that no one can question it. So it looks so solid and perfect that they'll believe it and just be happy for me.

On Sunday, I grab the grocery bag and Cyrus and I head out to his car.

"What's in there?" he asks, nodding his head at the bag as he pulls onto the road.

"Mom asked me to bring a dessert," I say, looking down at the box of cookies. "Which is funny, because she knows I can't cook. I think it was a little bit of payback for putting her off for so long."

He looks over at me, and it's there, more intense than usual. Like he's searching for answers on my face.

We drive across Greendale, and head into Cherico. I guide Cyrus through the main roads, and then the turn-off that cuts toward our neighborhood.

"I'm excited to meet them, your parents," Cyrus says as we turn onto my street. "I may not have much good to say about your biological mother, but she did right, doing what she did. Making that sacrifice. Despite the hardships you've had the last few years, you seem to love your family."

He parks in front of the house. And I feel my heart swell.

He's right.

I did have a good life. A good family.

I do love them.

So I have to do this. And I have to protect them.

"Are you ready?" he says, looking at me.

I stare into his beautiful face. So beautiful he isn't human. He isn't.

It's a face chiseled by time and trial and war and death.

But it's still beautiful.

I find myself leaning in just slightly. But he blinks, and shifts back ever so slightly.

"Yeah," I say.

I don't knock on the door, just let myself inside, and wonder how long it will be before I do it again. With Cyrus' hand held firmly in mine, I step inside.

The scent of pot roast is overwhelming. And warm rolls and stewing vegetables.

I swear my heart is going to beat right out of my chest as

I cross the front living room. And then round the corner into the dining room.

My grip on Cyrus' hand tightens involuntarily, but I am comforted when he squeezes back.

Three pairs of eyes immediately slide toward us, and my blood goes still.

"Logan," Mom grins from ear to ear as she wipes her hands on a towel and rushes across the room to wrap her arms around me. She squeezes tight, and I hug her back with just one arm, because I realize I'm too terrified to let go of Cyrus' hand.

"Hi, Mom," I breathe into her blonde hair. And I hug her long, not letting go for a few moments longer as she loosens her grip on me. Because I don't know how long it might be until I see her again.

"I'm so glad you came," she says quietly. And I realize just how much stress I have put her under the last few weeks as I dodged her requests.

I let her go and she backs up a step, taking Cyrus in.

"Mom, everyone," I breathe. "This is Collin."

King of the entire world of vampires.

"It's great to finally meet you," Cyrus says, stepping forward and wrapping Mom in a giant hug.

I have to look away for a second. I swear, these aren't tears trying to pool in my eyes.

"It's lovely to finally meet you," Mom glows as Cyrus releases her. There's a look in her eyes, it's the same one I see in nearly everyone's eyes when they look at Cyrus. He holds a power over women with that face of his. "So glad you could come have dinner with us."

"I wouldn't miss it for the world," Cyrus says with a wide, charming smile. "And you must be Ethan."

He steps forward, extending a hand toward my dad. He wheels in from the kitchen. And my heart nearly stops when Dad puts the brakes on the chair, and with shaking limbs, stands on his feet.

"It's a pleasure to meet you, Collin," Dad says. But he's certainly a dad. And he stares hard at Collin, as if chewing him out in his head, *how dare he move his daughter in with him so soon after meeting.*

"Collin," I say, stepping in to defuse the moment before it can grow too threatening, "this is my brother, Eshan."

He looks up from where he sits at the table on his phone. "Hey." He just gives a nod of his head.

"Eshan," Cyrus breathes. "Meaning ruler. Tell me, are you a man of power at your school?"

My brother looks up at Cyrus with a classic teenage look. Without a word, he just looks back down at his phone.

"You'll have to forgive his rudeness," Mom chides as she walks back into the kitchen. "We're dealing with classic cases of teenage angst with the approach of junior year."

"Let me make a guess," I say as I once more take Cyrus' hand and guide him toward the dining table. "There's a girl, and you know this is the year to make a move, and it's stressing you out?"

Eshan looks up and glares.

"What's her name?" I goad him.

"Go easy, Logan," Cyrus says as he pulls my chair out for me and slides it in. "A man is allowed to keep the desires of his heart close." He sits beside me, looping an arm over the back of my chair. "Let me give you some advice, Eshan."

And my brother actually looks at him. He's doubtful, but not entirely closed off.

"Make a woman feel like the most important part of your world, but never forget that she is still her own person," Cyrus says with absolute confidence. "For if you hold her too close, she will only want to roam."

"Some sage wisdom there," Dad says as he wheels over, setting a pitcher of water on the table. "How old are you again, Collin?"

"Twenty-seven," he lies without hesitation.

I can see it, the look of disapproval on my father's face. It's a big age difference, seven years, at least in his eyes. I suppose he's forgotten he and my mother have eight years between them.

Then again, I did just turn twenty a month and a half ago.

"Have you seen Eli recently?" Dad asks, changing the subject. "I haven't heard from him in a few weeks, and he hasn't stopped by."

My throat instantly tightens and I have to force myself not to glance in Cyrus' direction. "He's been out of town with work. Somewhere in Asia. He'll be back in about two weeks."

Dad nods, accepting my lie.

Again, I force myself not to look at Cyrus. But I'm so, so aware of every cell of his presence beside me.

"So, tell me," Mom says. "How did the two of you meet?" She sets the last of the food on the table and Eshan immediately digs in.

I look over at Cyrus, reminding him with my eyes to go along with whatever I say.

"I'd come home from dinner with Amelia," I say. It's easier to keep facts straight when they're blended slightly with the truth. "I'd gotten in a fight with Eli earlier, and went for a walk to clear my head. I honestly hadn't realized how late it was."

Part truth.

"There was this creepy guy lurking in an alley," I say. And I remember the glowing red eyes. The scream that came from my lungs.

"Collin stepped in and the guy ran away before it could go anywhere," I wrap it up with a big lie. "He took me out for coffee after that, and we just..." I look over at him and he meets my eyes. "Hit it off."

He reaches for my hand, lacing our fingers together.

He does it under the table, but it's obvious. Both my parents see the movement.

"Thank you," my dad pipes up. "For stepping in that night before anything could happen. I..." he shakes his head, at a loss for words for a moment. "It's a terrifying time of life, having your baby move out of your house, where you can't protect her all the time."

I look at Cyrus once more, and remember the night where he actually did protect me from a predator. "He's always there," I say. "Watching out for me."

"I promise you, Mr. Pierce, I won't ever let any harm come to Logan while she's with me."

It's a punch in the gut.

While I'm with him.

Because if I'm not who he's looking for, he's going to move on.

Everyone finishes dishing up and I put a bite into my mouth without tasting it.

"Thank you for dinner," Cyrus says. "Your cooking really is superb."

"Well, thank you, Collin," Mom says. And she actually blushes. "I love to cook. Unfortunately, I couldn't ever seem to teach Logan a thing. The poor thing can't even boil an egg."

"Mom," I gape in horror and embarrassment. "Really?"

"Yeah, Logan's not really good at much except playing with dead people," Eshan teases.

I look at my brother in horror. I could sock him right now. But at the same time I'm glad to see him finally relaxing tonight.

Mom just laughs, and everyone else smiles, too. "I'm sorry, honey. I swear I tried to prepare you to take care of yourself, but it just did not stick."

Cyrus smiles and looks over at me. "I suppose it's a good thing we have Fredrick."

"Fredrick?" Dad questions.

Cyrus looks back over, dabbing at the corner of his mouth with a napkin. "My assistant. He lives with us. He also cooks. Which is fortunate. Since neither Logan nor I know what to do when it comes to the kitchen."

"What do you do for work?" Dad asks, clearly interested in how Cyrus can afford an assistant.

And for a moment, I panic.

But I should have known Cyrus would be quick on his feet.

"I'm in politics," he says easily. "An ambassador, of sorts. My work takes me all around the world. It's what brought me here."

"So, you'll likely have to leave at some point?"

I hate that that's a hint of hope in Dad's voice.

"Actually," I pipe up. But my heart rate has tripled. Sweat breaks out onto my upper lip, my skin feels itchy. "I...I needed to talk to you all about something that's come up."

All at once, their eyes rise up and fix on me. Dad instantly goes ghost white. Mom looks worried. Eshan gives me a look with narrowed eyes.

"I've finished my school work," I say. I sit a little straighter, and push a little smile onto my lips. "But I've been wanting to learn more. I found this apprenticeship online. It teaches you all kinds of different embalming techniques. Mummification, desiccation, immersion. Things not commonly practiced anymore. Stuff I've been dying to learn."

Mom's expression sours. She hates it when I talk about my work.

"I applied," I say, making myself smile a little wider, "and I was accepted."

"Logan," Dad says, raising his glass to me. "That's great. Congratulations."

"It's just…" I hesitate. "It's in Austria. The apprenticeship lasts a year."

Cyrus' hand goes to my knee under the table and squeezes. I'm not exactly sure how to interpret it.

"Austria?" Mom chokes. "As in Europe?"

I nod, once more making myself smile. "And they've already got an apartment for me there and everything. I'll be studying under some really incredible people."

"Wow," Dad says, setting his glass down. "This sounds like an amazing opportunity for you, Logan."

I nod. Smile bigger. "It's really amazing. But…" I trail off, and everyone looks at me expectantly. "But I have to leave for it this coming weekend."

"What?" Mom gapes. "So soon?"

I nod. "I know it's sudden, and I'm sure going to miss everyone. But I'll never get another opportunity like this. And it's only a year. And then I'll be back, and there will be so many more opportunities for me then."

Dad smiles. It's sad. Doesn't quite reach his eyes. But still, he reaches across the table. "Good for you. I'm proud of you."

"Thanks," I smile.

Lies. All lies spewing from my mouth.

"And what does that mean for you two?" Mom asks, looking from me to Cyrus. "Surely the both of you know how difficult long distance is?"

"As it so happens," Cyrus says, looking in my direction.

"My work is taking me to Austria for a time. And from there, we'll see what happens."

He leans forward, pressing a gentle kiss to my forehead.

And my body rips with confusion and excitement.

"Gross," Eshan says, shaking his head. "That's my sister."

And it was just what we needed. Cyrus laughs. Dad laughs. Mom laughs.

And so I do, too.

∼

CYRUS IS A FREAKING CHARMER.

A snake when he's in the political arena.

A family wooing, compliment slinging, belly-laugh inducing charmer in my family's house.

Where Dad was wary and unsure of Cyrus when we walked in, by the end of the night, he's sitting on the couch and they're both laughing about this or that like they've been friends for years. Even Eshan laughs and cracks jokes at my expense with them.

Mom and I sit at the dining table after the dishes have been loaded. She watches the boys, her feet propped up on a chair.

"I think you found a good one, Logan," Mom says quietly. She watches Cyrus' who laughs loudly at something Dad says. "Anyone who can make your father laugh like that… And I've never seen you look at anyone the way you look at him."

I don't know what to say. There's so much she doesn't know.

But Mom isn't the first one to say this.

And hearing it… This is dangerous. I can't fall for Cyrus. I just can't.

"He's done something for you, Logan," Mom says. She reaches across the table and takes my hand. "I don't know what it is, but you're just…lighter, in a way, than you have been in a long while. I'm glad you've found someone who makes you so happy."

"Thanks, Mom," I say through a tight throat.

The hour grows late. Nine o'clock. At ten o'clock my parents send Eshan to bed, which really means he's just going to go watch TV in his room. I hug him goodnight. Goodbye.

I'm really going to miss the moody little prick.

For an hour the adults sit in the living room. Cyrus plays his part well, tucking me into his side, wrapping one arm around my shoulders, holding my hand. And it's just a natural fit, sitting with my legs over his lap. He twirls a finger through my hair.

Every moment of the night is pain. Every connection of my skin to his. Every fake loving look he gives my way.

I fall. Down a dark well with no end in sight. But all that can wait at the bottom of it is sharp spikes.

"Are you tired?" Cyrus asks quietly as the night grows darker outside and the hour pushes past eleven.

I shrug, giving him a sleepy little smile for my parent's sake.

"I know I am," Mom says with a dramatic yawn. "As much as I love having you here, I think I'm going to have to give in and head to bed."

Cyrus climbs to his feet and pulls me to mine, holding onto my hand.

"Thank you, so much, for having us over," he says, smiling at my parents. Dad shakily gets to his feet, standing behind his wheelchair, bracing himself with it. Mom stands and hugs the both of us.

"It was a pleasure, Collin," she says with a broad grin. "I expect pictures from the both of you when you get to Austria."

"Promise," I say, and realize it's likely one I won't be keeping.

With goodbyes that shred my heart into a thousand pieces, we end the night.

As we walk down the sidewalk to the car, I look back over my shoulder.

"It won't be the last time," Cyrus says quietly. "You'll be able to see them again."

I nod. "But it will never be quite the same again."

Cyrus takes my hand and I look back at him. He raises it to press a kiss to my knuckles.

This one isn't for show. Not for my family. Not for Amelia.

"It isn't an easy thing, to have one's life totally changed," he says quietly, staring at me fervently with his green eyes. "Human's thrive on normalcy. They crave it. You thought normal was going to be your life. Were you not born to a vast destiny, you could have lived this life."

But in the back of my mind, the words echo, *but then I never would have met you.*

I give him a sad little nod, and together we climb into the car.

CHAPTER 19

MONDAY.

One final week.

Seven days.

I'm an emotional wreck. A ball of anticipation. Of wrecked feelings. Of racing thoughts and moments of numb despair.

"Get out of the damn way!" I scream at the car in front of me on the way to work. I lay on the horn, but it doesn't make the driver any smarter. They continue blocking the lane they shouldn't have pulled into with all this traffic.

Finally, ten minutes late, I pull into the parking lot of Sykes Funeral Home.

My hands quake violently as I walk to Emmanuel's office. My voice shakes as I tell him I need to talk to him. I'm pretty sure I'm going to puke as I tell him about my fake apprenticeship in Austria.

He sits there silently for a minute when I finish telling him these are my final five days at work. He stares at me with hard eyes.

"Austria?" he questions. "Not the catacombs in Rome? Not the mummifiers in Egypt? Austria."

My heart drops into my stomach with an acidic splash.

"Yes," I say, forcing myself to sound confident. "At St. Margaret de Tod."

Emmanuel keeps staring at me. But slowly, so slowly I'm pretty sure I'm going to die from dread that he's going to see the holes in my story, his face relaxes.

"Well," he finally says. "I can't say I'm happy you're only giving me a week's notice." He stands. "But I suppose you didn't get much choice. And," he stops in front of me, "it sounds like it will be an incredible opportunity for you."

A smile breaks out onto my face, and I let out a breath of relief when he wraps his arms around me in a hug.

The next step in saying goodbye to my human life: check.

I text Amelia after work that day and ask if I can come over for a few minutes. Once more feeling sick, I head to her new apartment.

She cries. When I tell her, Amelia isn't exactly happy for me and doesn't understand why I'd want to learn how to completely desiccate a body to preserve it for centuries, because that's just disgusting. She buries her face in my chest and just cries.

"It'll only be for a year," I comfort her. "I swear, when I'm done, we'll go on an epic road trip. To California or Florida or somewhere warm with an ocean."

"We better," she sobbed.

Feeling hollow and tired, I head back to the house that night.

The moment I walk in the door, it's obvious everything is wrong.

"Were there not security cameras installed before we purchased the home?" I hear Cyrus bellow.

I step into the living room, and my blood goes cold.

The house has been tossed. The furniture is all out of sorts. All the bookcases have been toppled. Everything from the kitchen has been drug out and the cupboards look like they exploded.

"What…" my voice shakes. "What the hell happened?"

Sharp eyes turn to me. Cyrus, glowing red. Mina, with fear and shame. Fredrick with just terror.

"Apparently the security here was not as up to par as we were led to believe," Cyrus hisses. "It was what it looks like."

Like someone broke in and went searching the house for…something. And dug through every square inch of the house to find it.

"What were they looking for?" I ask, looking around.

A low rumble echoes from Cyrus' chest. I look over, to see him glaring with red eyes at Mina.

"Confirmation," he says.

"Of what?" I question.

"That I am here!" he bellows. "That the King has indeed arrived once more in America and has been operating for weeks under little to no security."

"Who?" I demand. "Who would do this? Why would they be looking for you?"

Cyrus swings, smacking a glass from the counter. It smashes against the fridge, denting the appliance, and sending shards of glass spraying throughout the kitchen.

"One does not rule this long without making hundreds of enemies," he growls. Abruptly he turns and stalks toward me. "I am sorry, Logan, but I'm afraid I can no longer hold up my end of the deal. We must do this now and leave."

I back up, but he's too fast. He darts forward, grabbing my wrist. His eyes glow bright.

"No!" I scream. "You said you were a man of your word. Do you really want to destroy that now over someone I know you can hold your own against?"

Black veins slowly creep out over Cyrus' face and his eyes flare brighter for just a moment.

Hot rage bubbles in my chest.

"Are you afraid?" I taunt.

He hisses, low and rumbling.

"The King may have many enemies, but he has not remained King by running with his tail between his legs over a tossed house." I stand straight, yanking my wrist out of his grip.

Bravado. I gather it all up inside me to fight back the rising panic.

My death is seconds away at any moment. Cyrus is certainly capable.

If I'm going to fight for my last moments, I have to do it with certainty.

"Seven days," Cyrus hisses. "You will die in seven days. But be prepared for some ugly, tumultuous ones."

He turns, and yells at Fredrick and Mina in German. They go scurrying.

I turn, and head for my bedroom, which has been just as thoroughly ransacked as the rest of the house.

CHAPTER 20

Something has changed.

Where Cyrus used to look at me with want in his eyes, like he could will who he wishes me to be into life, he's withdrawn. Hasty. He's done waiting.

When I get home from work on Tuesday, he asks me if he can end it today.

I tell him no.

On Wednesday he asks me the same.

I tell him it isn't yet time.

It's fear that holds me back. It's the uncertainty that I will indeed rise from the dead after lying there for four days.

What if he's wrong?

He seems so certain. But what if I am the exception to this supernatural rule?

What if I just stay dead?

Only to forget everything, to be reborn somewhere else in the world?

On Thursday, I walk through the door. The house has been put back together, and Mina is nowhere to be found. Security from the House of Valdez arrived Tuesday morning. She's been busy with them setting up perimeters and keeping watch for whoever it was that broke into the house.

So it's just Cyrus who sits at the head of the dining table.

"You have said your goodbyes already," he says darkly. I walk through the entryway, entering into the room, my jaw set hard. My eyes narrowed. "You've given your notice at work. What are these mere days at the end?"

I slam my bag down on the table. "They are my choice," I growl. I put my hands on the back of the chair. "These last few days, they are my choice. After I die, I don't know how much of a choice in my life I am going to have. I don't know what my life is going to be like after. But I do know what to expect in the next few days."

My breathing rips in and out, hard. My knuckles are white from holding onto the chair.

"People must have choice, Cyrus," I say, forcing my voice to calm. "There has to be free will. You can't take away all of my choice."

Like I slapped him physically, Cyrus sits back in his chair, away from me. He stares at me with wide, surprised eyes.

We stare at one another in silence for a long moment. I won't back down. I won't apologize.

I know he won't, either.

But I won't be the first to bend.

Cyrus stands, his chair scraping the floor loudly as he pushes it back.

He looks over at me one more time. And then he walks to the stairs, and silently leaves.

Arrogant, bullying, bossy, hotheaded prick, I seethe as I stalk up the stairs a minute later. I change, throwing on stretchy, breathable clothes.

Don't think, I tell myself as I plug my headphones in and walk out the front door a few minutes later.

I crank my music as loud as it will go, and I run.

It was bright when I left. Hot. Sweat pours down my back as I run and I run, and I don't think about anything but the pounding and screaming in my ears.

It's getting dark when I get back to the house. Keeping my head low, determined to tune all the drama out, I shower and go downstairs to find something to eat.

There's half a pizza in a box, probably bought from one of the security people of the House of Valdez. But I take two slices and warm them up in the microwave.

Feeling moody and annoyed and sad and a little broken, I eat them while looking out over the back yard.

A plan.

I need to come up with a plan.

Because if Cyrus leaves me, I have to decide where I want to go.

Consider your mother, Edmond had said.

But I remember that card with my name on it upstairs in my room.

Considering what Cyrus said I will be like for the first few months, holding a job is going to be impossible. I'll kill my coworkers, expose the vampires. I'll have no choice but to live off of Cyrus' money.

Travel. Maybe I'll just travel non-stop. I'll see the world.

But that sounds incredibly lonely. Having no one to share it with me.

The food in my mouth loses its taste. I toss the rest in the trash and put the plate in the dishwasher.

Feeling too heavy, but too empty, I walk up the stairs. I turn to head to my bedroom.

But the utter silence coming from the bedroom with the open door pulls my eyes to it.

The bedroom is meticulously clean and organized. The bed is made, and I'm pretty sure it hasn't been slept in for over a week. The doors to the closet and bathroom remain propped open.

There, standing at the window, with only a towel slung around his hips, is Cyrus. He has his hands braced on the ledge of the window, slightly bent over.

He's so quiet. So utterly still.

And the tenseness in his shoulders tells me this is a man with the weight of the world upon them.

"Cyrus?" I say quietly, taking half a step inside.

He doesn't flinch. He doesn't even take a breath in. Nothing that acknowledges my presence.

I take another step inside. "Are you..." I trail off. Because it's a stupid question with a very obvious answer that he is not all right. I walk in, coming to his right side, his face coming into view.

His hair is wet, hanging down in his face. It drips, slowly, running down his face.

His entire body is wet, as if he didn't dry any bit of himself off.

He doesn't look at me, just stands there frozen, staring outside. His eyes are empty. Hollow. Mentally, he's a million miles away.

And it cracks me.

I've been angry with this man the last few days. I've gotten tired of his demands for my death. I have no patience left for his commands that everyone but me jumps to fulfill. I'm tired of the way he's been distant and removed ever since the dinner with my family. So I've put up a wall the last few days.

But seeing that look in his eyes.

My heart aches for him.

"Cyrus," I breathe. I reach forward, touching his bare shoulder.

His skin is freezing cold. I wonder how long ago he got out of the shower and has just been standing here, dripping wet.

He tenses slightly, the only indication he knows I'm here.

"Cyrus, please talk to me," I say. I push against his shoulder, breaking the grip of his right hand on the window, and pushing myself in front of him. He stands, and I remain there, face to face with him.

Emptily, he continues to stare out the window.

"Tell me what you want," I whisper. I raise my hands to his face, one on each cheek. Tenderly, I guide his head, trying to make him look at me. "Cyrus, please tell me what would make you happy."

It fractures me further when his eyes well just a little with emotion. His face pales, but he doesn't look away from the window.

"Cyrus, please talk to me," I breathe.

It's building inside of me. Rising with the force of a freight train. Bubbling and building to the surface, threatening to drown me. I've been trying to hold onto logic for weeks now. To argue with myself into behaving rationally.

But staring into his hollow green eyes, reason is gone.

I can't fight the truth in my chest any more.

"Cyrus," I whisper again. I tip my head forward, resting my forehead against his collarbone, feeling my own emotions rushing to the surface. I want to hold him, for him to hold me. I want to hear his voice and for him to whisper my name in my ear.

But he just stands there.

I huff a deep breath, broken and cracked sounding.

"I want to know what you want," I say, letting my lips brush against the skin of his chest.

It kills me. Because I realize now what it is that I want.

But I realize now, that I won't have it.

And it's going to entirely wreck me.

So it's a move of self-preservation when I take a step away. I barely hold back the tears as I separate our contact.

But a lightning quick hand darts out, catching my wrist.

"Wait," Cyrus whispers.

I stand there, frozen, my back to him.

"What I want..." he trails off. And there is a lifetime of emotions in those words. He pauses for a long time and my heart breaks for him. Cyrus is a man constantly surrounded by people. People who do unnatural things to please him. People who bend to his will and command.

But Cyrus is the loneliest man I've ever met.

"Please stay," he breathes.

Slowly, I turn. He still stares out the window, and he's still hollow. But one of those tears has broken free. Slowly, it slides down his cheek. It clings at his jawline. But it doesn't have the strength to hold on. It falls to the carpet at our feet.

I slide my hand into his, and he clings on tight. I raise it, clutching it to my chest, where he can feel my heart thundering against my ribcage. Slowly, I back toward the bed, and he follows me, never looking into my face.

But for this night, it's okay. On this night, I can take care of a broken man. A man who changed the world. A man who could command it. Tonight, I see it in his eyes. He needs a strong heart and a soft touch.

I pull him into the bed behind me. He lies down and I pull the covers up over the both of us.

He rolls toward me, and without hesitation, he buries his face into my neck, his arms wrapping around me.

For just a moment, my heart stumbles. His lips are against my neck, and just behind them, I know are sharp, life-ending fangs. All it would take is one bite, long pulls, and I would be dead, just how he wants.

But he only clings to me.

So I wrap my arms around the King. My hands caress his strong back. I twine my legs around his, holding him close.

Cyrus doesn't say another word. He just clings to me as tight as he can, not even breathing.

And I know.

He doesn't breathe, because it's too painful.

So I hold King Cyrus.

And finally, sometime later, he falls asleep in my arms.

CHAPTER 21

THE PILLOW UNDER MY HEAD TWITCHES. IT'S HARD, AND shaped wrong.

I roll, my brows furrowing in confusion.

I open my eyes, and find myself nose to nose with a sleeping Cyrus.

His ever-furrowed brows, always tense with stress or power, are finally relaxed. His lips are slightly parted. His head rests on his pillow, his arm extended out.

It was his arm I'm lying on.

His other is draped over my side. He shifts, his leg draping over mine, pinning me down. Holding me close.

I blink, slow, tired. I study his dark eyelashes. His hair is wild, standing on end, draped over his forehead. It's thick. So thick, it's all I can do to keep my fingers from running through it.

My heart rate increases. But I tell myself to keep it under control. The last thing I want is for it to wake him up.

Enjoy this while it lasts, I think to myself.

I relish the contact. My skin to his skin. Lying here as if he is mine. One unpleasant person tangled up in the arms and legs of another unpleasant person.

Contentedly, I let a little sigh loose.

Cyrus' eyes flutter open. Slowly, he blinks.

A tiny smile pulls on my lips, and my insides flutter when his eyes are not empty this morning.

Slowly, he raises a hand up and cups the side of my face, his fingers splaying into my hair.

"Are you a dream?" he breathes, searching my eyes.

I shake my head slightly. "No."

His search deepens. "Do you ever dream of me?"

My heart rate picks up. "Almost every night."

My pulse doubles at that look in his eyes.

Emotions rage through me at lightning speed. The crack of thunder roars in my ears as I reach up, holding onto Cyrus' wrist.

And I give up the fight as I lean forward, letting my eyes slide closed.

Like falling as you fall asleep, I startle back, because suddenly there is no body beside mine.

"What do you think you are doing?" a growl sounds from the opposite side of the room.

I startle, blinking fast, searching for Cyrus.

He stands beside the door, quickly trying to secure the towel from last night around his waist once again.

His eyes glow brilliant red, rage and disgust on his face.

"I…" I stutter. "Cyrus, I-"

"Who do you think you are, to be so presumptuous?" he growls as he marches to the closet. He closes it most of the way and I hear him yanking through the hangers. Raging through drawers. "What gives you the audacity to think you can kiss the King?"

My mouth hangs open as I shift, kneeling on the bed we shared last night. "Cyrus, I don't-"

He stalks out of the closet. He wears a pair of jeans, still unbuttoned, showing his black underwear. But he does not wear a shirt.

"It is not your place," he seethes, his eyes narrowed and burning.

"Who the hell do you think you are?" I demand as my blood begins to boil. "You can't look at a woman the way you look at me, you can't hold me the way you've held me, without a woman thinking you might want her."

His eyes burn with anger, but also something…else. But his lips remain pressed into a thin line.

"I need you to be very clear with me, Cyrus," I say, my volume lessening just slightly. "You want something from me. You want me to be someone. I see it in your eyes every time you look at me. I feel it every time you've touched me. You're waiting to see if I'm…I don't know. And it's confusing the hell out of me. Because…" I hesitate, feeling the energy drain out of me. "Because there is something growing between us. And I can't deny the ache in my chest anymore. I can't handle the idea of the possible coming separation. So, I need you to tell me, exactly, who you want me to be."

"I want you to be my wife!" Cyrus bellows, his eyes flaring brilliant. He swings an arm through the air with an exclamation. "I want to *finally* not be alone. I want to finally, finally be together once more."

Everything in me stills. Stops racing. Stops raging with confusion and desire.

"Wife?" I question.

The both of us finally slow. Just staring at one another.

As the honest truth begins to come out.

"I have been hoping, hoping against all hope," Cyrus breathes, the intake rough and jagged, "that you are her."

My hands shake. I grip the white blankets below to try and tame it. But it doesn't help the trembling. "What…what is that supposed to mean?"

The fight seems to seep out of Cyrus. His shoulders sag. His head hangs forward and the breath seeps out of his chest.

"It means," he says, "that I have never, ever kissed another woman besides my wife." He takes a step forward, and then another. "It means, that for 286 years, I have been alone. It means, that for 286 years, I have searched for her." He drops to his knees at the foot of the bed, his eyes fixed on mine. "It means, that for the past twenty-seven days, I have prayed that you will be her."

My body is very cold. Surely my heart has stopped. It isn't pushing blood through my body anymore.

I shake my head, as emotions fill my eyes. "I don't understand."

His head drops and he shakes his head.

"I loved my wife, more than anything in this world," he says. "But I did not realize it until after I achieved immortality. I did not realize it until after I took her free will and turned her against her choice."

He grips the edge of the bed, as if holding on for dear life. As if he might fall straight down to hell if he were to let go.

"I cursed myself then, not only with the craving of blood," he says. "But I cursed myself to lose that which I valued most." He takes one deep, ragged breath. "After only eighty-nine years of immortality together, my wife grew sick. She was frail. There wasn't enough blood in the world to sate her thirst. And after only weeks of this, she died."

He trembles, quaking. As if the story he tells will wreck him.

"But then, fifty-one years later, a descendant of Malachi died. And just a week after she Resurrected, she came to the castle. She said my name. And she knew. Everything. Everything of our past. Of our lives together. It was my wife, reborn. Once more returned to me."

The bed trembles from his grip, as he quakes.

And I grow colder. I'm frozen. Rooted as if I have turned to stone.

"But once more, after one hundred and fifty-three years, she grew ill again." His words are quiet. As if he can barely breathe. "Once more, the love of my very long, immortal life, died."

Cyrus' words echo around my head, as if bouncing

against the hard inside of my skull. Knocking, hard, saying, *hello? Can you hear me? Are you there?*

"Over and over and over again, my wife would be reborn somewhere in the Royal bloodline. Around the globe. Always with a different face. Always awakening to remembrance after Resurrecting. And she would always die again and again in my arms."

The dancers at the House of Valdez. The story they told of that Queen. It was the story of Cyrus' wife. It was the reason he reacted in such a violent way.

My hands shake. But slowly, I raise them, looking down at them.

Edmond Valdez made a call to King Cyrus.

I understand that doesn't mean she's anything but human, but I'm asking you to consider the fact that this man is here guarding her. That has to mean something. And considering it's the House of Conrath? From what I hear, he and their leader have some...interesting history.

"For centuries, longer, I have made sure to keep close tabs on all of the male Royals, and any offspring they may produce. So that is the reason I flew from across the world to meet you, Logan."

When he says my name, my body loses strength. I can barely keep myself sitting upright.

"That is why when I tasted your blood, confirmed you were indeed a female descendant of a male Royal, I wished for your immediate death."

"Because in four days, I would Resurrect, and you would know."

Finally, Cyrus raises his head, and he looks me in the eye. "In four days, I could know."

Wife. *Wife.*

I could be someone I have forgotten.

I could be Cyrus' wife.

The world. The entire vampire world, the entire House of Valdez. Eli—Rath. They *all* know.

That is why they all have been watching me so close this entire time.

"Why did you not tell me sooner?" I ask. My voice shakes. With confusion. With betrayal. With embarrassment. "This has gotten so complicated and tangled and now I... Why didn't you tell me right away who you hoped I was?"

Emotion pools in my eyes. But as I meet Cyrus', I see them harden.

His jaw tightens.

His fingers clench harder around the blankets on the bed.

"Why?" I ask.

"Because sixteen years ago," he says, his voice barely controlled. "I came to America to meet another female descendant. That of my enemy, Henry Conrath. A woman who had no knowledge of her birthright, of her world. But once she learned of it, she rose to her station and owned it well, even as a human."

My heart drops into my stomach and I feel my expression slacken.

I know where this story is going.

And I think I finally understand.

"Sixteen years ago, I went to the House of Conrath with

very, very high hopes. That after all this time, perhaps this woman would be the one." A wicked smile curls on Cyrus' lips. "And heartbroken Alivia, who had been forsaken by her love, she saw that hope in my eyes."

My own hands tighten around the blanket. Tighten, wrinkling the fabric. My fingernails dig into my palms through it.

"Alivia played me," Cyrus says through his teeth. "With the expertise of a slithering snake. She whispered in my ear about time and castles. She pulled me close and looked at me as if I were the sun and she a blooming rose."

Cyrus' eyes are unfocused, burning with rage.

"Alivia nearly broke me with hope." His voice drops quiet. Empty.

I can feel his pain. So plain and laid bare.

"She let me believe," he says. "She encouraged me, laid her head upon my chest and dared whisper the name husband."

I squeeze my eyes closed, wishing he would take back the words.

"All while she snuck behind my back with my most trusted spy." His words are a whisper, so filled with betrayal. "All while her heart still longed for Ian Ward. She let me hope. And in the end, it broke the both of us."

His head snaps up, and I quake from fear when his eyes meet mine.

I see it there. I *know* it.

He punished my mother for what she did.

"So, I swore I wouldn't do it again," Cyrus shakes his head. "I would not let myself be led along by another. So, I did not tell you and commanded that no other would. So that you would be yourself and never try to toy with my heart."

But his expression softens. He rises to his feet.

"I may not have been kind these past few days, Logan," Cyrus says. Once more, I see it, how draining this information is. "But you..." he shakes his head, his eyes sliding closed. "You are slowly driving me mad. The things you say, the person you are..."

He takes in a deep breath, and I try to understand his meaning.

"I cannot take it any longer, Logan," he says. Emotion tugs on his words. "I must know. Please," he whispers. "Please end this uncertainty for me."

I crawl across the bed slowly. When I reach the end of it, I rise up onto my knees. I place a hand on either side of his face, and slowly his eyes open.

Dark green. Deep as the ocean. Ancient as the forest.

"The last month has been an incredible, unforgettable one," I say. Our faces are so close. We breathe the same air. I feel the heat of him. "And I never expected it, the way you'd twist my stomach up and confuse every emotion in me."

His eyes slide closed and his hands rise to rest on my hips.

"I realized it last night, and just now, my heart told me the truth," I whisper as it fractures. "I wanted you to love me for me. And for you to stop looking for someone else whenever you look in my eyes."

I press my lips to Cyrus' forehead as he stops breathing.

I squeeze my eyes closed. A tear pushes out onto

my cheek.

Before I can shatter apart on this bed, I climb off and walk toward the door.

"Logan," Cyrus calls.

I stop with my hand on the door and look over my shoulder.

He stares after me, the face of an anguished, confused man greeting me.

I watch him, waiting for him to say the words. To tell me that he does love me, no matter who I may turn out to be.

His wife or not.

But he can't seem to find any more words.

So I open that door, and I walk out.

IT'S FRIDAY. MY VERY LAST DAY OF WORK AT SYKES Funeral Home.

No one died last night, so there isn't any work for me to do. Instead Emmanuel went and got a cake, and as a send-off, he, Craig, and Katie throw me a little going away party. I try my best not to, but as I gather my few personal belongings and hug each of them goodbye, I cry.

I look around my workspace, and I know it: I'm going to miss this, what I do, very, very much. Because somehow I know, I'll never work as a mortician again.

Everything will change.

That afternoon, I sit in my car for a very long time, trying to decide what to do. Trying to decide how I feel.

Cyrus has been searching my face, overthinking everything I say, because he's been watching for signs of his Resurrecting wife.

The acknowledgement of that truth sends shivers racing down my arms.

It's why he has said my fate after I Resurrected wouldn't be determined until the act was done.

If I am his wife, we'll have a happily ever after, for a time, and I will return to *Roter Himmel* with him.

If I am not her, he doesn't really care where I go.

Rath—he's been watching over me nearly my entire life. Because once Alivia Conrath realized my father was a Royal, she understood that one day, the King would indeed come to find me. So she sent Rath to watch over me.

Alivia and Cyrus have a dark, twisted relationship.

I think I somewhat understand.

But the King... The man who took my acid... The man who killed a man to protect me...

Emotion instantly rips through me, and a sob escapes my lips before I can stop it. Tears well into my eyes and slide down my face.

I've fallen in love with Cyrus over the past month. I tried to fight it. Told myself it was insane and stupid considering how he came into my life; the way he took control over it.

But it happened. One intense gaze at a time. One charming encounter with those I care about it at a time. One act of heroism at a time.

Maybe I'm weak minded. Maybe I'm an embarrassment to all women. But it's the truth.

I fell hopelessly, soul-endingly in love with King Cyrus.

A man I can never keep unless I am someone I don't remember.

Sobbing, I drive my way over to Amelia's apartment. With trembling fingers, I text her.

Are you home?

Just watching TV. What's up?

Come outside.

Three seconds later, her head pops out of their door.

I lose it the second I see her and with a panicked look, she darts into the passenger seat of my car.

"Where is he?" she demands. "Point me in the right direction and I will slaughter him."

I cry harder and shake my head as I collapse into her arms.

"What is it, Lo?" Amelia asks, running her hand down the back of my hair. "What happened?"

"I wasn't…" I sob. "I wasn't supposed to love him. It wasn't supposed to turn real."

"Real?" she questions, her hand stilling. "What is that supposed to mean?"

I shake my head again as tears stream down my face. "I knew who he was, right from the beginning. And I still fell in love with him."

"Duh, Lo," Amelia chuckles. "It's been pretty obvious for a while. You're in deep. What's so bad about that?"

I shake my head, letting every emotion pour out of me. "Because there's a good chance that in just a few days, our lives are going to permanently go separate ways."

I'm out of my mind. I realize I can't answer all of her questions, that to her, none of this is going to make sense.

"Just because his work isn't taking him to Austria anymore, doesn't mean it has to end. Nothing bad has happened, has it?" she asks.

I don't know what to say. She doesn't understand everything, she assumes wrongly. "No. The way things are going to go…it's something that isn't either of our faults. But it's still going to wreck me."

Amelia thinks for a moment, and slowly, she brushes her hand down my hair again. "Love wrecks us. And even if you do go your separate ways, it doesn't mean that love ends. Maybe it's just easier if you still love them, and be happy for what might come for them in the future. And tell yourself that when the time is right, that you're allowed to be happy again."

Her words sink into my heart, and begin to calm my raging storm. I take a slow breath, and sit up. "Why do you get to be so smart *and* so damn pretty?"

She gives me a sad little smile. She reaches forward and wipes my tears with her thumb. "I don't know exactly what's going on. You've kind of been keeping me in the dark when it comes to your first time love life." We both chuckle at that. "But I know when you love someone, you fight for them. Even if there's a chance you might not win. You're a fighter, Lo. So go fight."

I reach forward, holding her hand, and squeezing on for strength. "Thank you."

She smiles. "Any time. Even if you're about to be half

way around the world."

I smile sadly, hating that I have to keep letting her believe the lie. "I love you."

"I love you, too," she says as she pulls me in for a hug.

Tanner pops his head out of the door and Amelia lets me go. "Call me when you get to your new place."

"I will when I can," I say, the only promise I can make her.

She waves and climbs out, and walks back into her apartment with her normal boyfriend and her normal life.

I sit there for a minute longer, contemplating everything she just said.

It's too hard. I don't want to accept it. To be the grown up who can have such an adult frame of mind.

But this is my life. And it's rushing at me with supersonic speed.

With a deep breath, I put the car into drive, and I head home.

When I arrive, it seems quiet. Though I know most of the House of Valdez has been in the shadows, watching the perimeter, I don't see any traces of them. Looking around, I get out of my car and head to the front door.

"Has the repairman arrived yet?" Fredrick says, looking out the door as soon as I walk in.

"Repairman?" I question as I set my box of things on the table.

"The internet," Fredrick says. "It went out yesterday afternoon. The company is supposed to be sending someone to fix it today."

"And that doesn't seem suspicious to you all?" I say, raising an eyebrow.

"Of course it is," Fredrick says, though his accent is so thick, it's a struggle to understand any of his words. "Do not think that we won't be on high alert."

My heart rate jumps. "I assume Cyrus isn't here with the risk."

Fredrick looks back at me and glares. "Your challenge seems to have gone to his head. He refused to leave as a precaution."

That was in fact my doing. But still, sweat breaks out onto my palms.

A utility van drives up just then, bright colors and words painted all over the side of it. As a man climbs out, I hear the trees and bushes rustle, and know the Valdez crew has stirred to action.

The man grabs a bag from the back and walks up to the door where Fredrick and I stand waiting.

"Afternoon," he greets casually with the tip of his hat.

Fredrick doesn't say a word, but I see his nostrils flare. He takes a deep inhale, smelling the man without being obvious.

I cover, giving a greeting.

"The equipment is in the living room," Fredrick says stiffly. "I'll accompany you."

The man nods and heads into the house.

"Human," Fredrick whispers as he follows the man.

I look out the door, searching for signs of the guards, but see none. I close the door, and wander back inside.

The repairman searches through a cabinet where the equipment is, quietly speaking with Fredrick. I can feel the tension, rolling through the house like waves. I wonder how many guards are inside, hiding where I cannot see them.

Satisfied that the repairman is nothing but that, I turn and head up the stairs.

Somewhere in this house is Cyrus. Being stubborn and arrogant. Demanding he can take care of himself.

Ugh. That stupid man makes my heart twist into knots.

I turn down the hall, about to head for my bedroom, when a slight squeak draws my eye to the closet across the hall from Cyrus' bedroom.

Fight or flight. My nerves kick into high gear.

I look around, searching for anything to use as a weapon. I settle for a candlestick on the table in the hall. It's heavy, solid metal.

I press myself flat against the wall when the door swings open, this time without making a sound.

Thunder. Roar.

My instincts go wild.

A tiny form of a shadow emerges from the closet.

Just then, the door to Cyrus' bedroom swings open and Cyrus takes half a step out. "Logan, is that you?"

I started diving the second I saw the door opening. A sprint. A giant leap.

Because I saw that hand swing.

I saw the sharp tip of a stake.

Amelia's words rip through my head as I jump. *Maybe*

it's just easier if you still love them, and be happy for what might come for them in the future.

I don't even get to look at his face. I just jump, wildly swinging the candlestick.

I hit them hard in the neck with a thump.

But the tip of the stake buries itself into my chest.

With a scream, I collide to the floor, my eyes fixated on the face of a man. Dark blonde hair. A longer, unkempt beard. And his eyes glow red with hatred.

A roar echoes throughout the entire house. An injured lion out for blood. A demon from another world.

The breath catches in my throat. I try to suck in air, but the feeling is all wrong.

Blood warms my chest.

The man is tackled to the floor instantly and Cyrus is a wild, rabid animal. Shedding. Ripping. Teeth flashing.

The attacker gets one muffled scream before it's cut off with a gurgled blub.

Feet pound on the stairs and down the hallway.

Faces swarm, but all I can feel is pain.

My hands trembling, I search for the stake.

It's buried in my chest, on the right side. Angled inward from the fleshy part where my arm and chest meet.

I can't breathe.

I can't get any air.

"Logan," Cyrus' face suddenly appears in my vision. He's panic stricken, his face bone white, a stark contrast to his glowing red eyes and the blood sprayed across it. "Logan, why...why did you do that?"

I feel his arms slide under me and he lifts. A scream of pain rips from my chest, which causes more pain. I scream some more.

Gently, Cyrus lays me on his bed. His hands fuss around, hovering over the stake.

Other faces swim into the corners of my vision, but it's darker where they are.

I keep looking at Cyrus, trying not to think about how I can't breathe.

"She must have a collapsed lung," a voice says. I think it's Mina.

"How did he get in?" Cyrus growls, looking up at the others.

"The day we found the house in shambles," she says. "I think...I think perhaps they never actually left the house."

"Your Majesty," another voice says, one I do not recognize. "They had been waiting for you. That stake in her chest was meant for your heart."

Cyrus eyes drop back down to mine. He takes my hand, holding it up to his mouth. "Why?" he breathes. "Why would you do this, Logan?"

Tears well in my eyes. My lip trembles. "You know why," I whisper. One tear breaks free from my eyes and rolls down my face.

He leans forward, pressing his forehead to mine. And I realize that he is shaking.

"At least you get what you want now," I breathe. My chest hurts. My brain is screaming for more oxygen.

"No," Cyrus says, shaking his head. "Not like this. It

should never have ended in terror and fear."

With my left hand, I reach up, lacing my fingers through his hair. "Better me than you. Had he gotten you, it would have been the end, and I..." The breath runs out of my lungs and I can't pull any more words.

Cyrus shakes his head, and it makes me think that perhaps he doesn't think it true.

"Logan, I..." his voice trembles. He falters, and my heart hurts even more for him when I see the confusion in his eyes. "Thank you. I am grateful to have the time finally arrive," he whispers. He looks into my eyes. "So I can finally stop feeling guilty."

"Guilty?" I manage just one more word.

He stares at me, and finally I see something different in his eyes. Me. Just me.

"The guilt of feeling as if I am betraying my wife," he whispers. His words sound far away. The world grows a little darker. "Because when I look at you, Logan...."

Peace. It settles into my chest, overriding the pain. Taking over the fear and panic riding through me.

A small smile pulls on my lips.

Even as the strength seeps out of me. My hand falls away from his face, flopping to the bed, useless.

"I understand if I'm not her and you need to keep search-ing," I say. I finally accept what I've been so terrified of. "I pray you find her."

Tears well into Cyrus' eyes and one breaks free, landing on my jawline.

"You deserve to find peace, Cyrus," I whisper, knowing

my words are running out. I let my eyes slide closed. "I'm ready."

He hesitates. For a few moments. And in that hesitation, the pain and the suffocation come roaring back. Like a black, inky monster. It spreads from the stake, stretching out to every corner of my body.

But then there's another pain.

A sharp bite. Fangs latching onto my neck, just over my carotid artery.

And then pulls. Long, strong pulls as Cyrus sucks my blood from my body.

Numbness spreads from the bite, and I nearly sigh in relief. My brain fogs and I stop caring about anything.

Pull after pull.

The world grows quieter.

The pain becomes less.

Deeper into the darkness I slip, eagerly embracing its welcome.

But somewhere in the back of my mind, I feel the sensation of fangs retreating.

Deeper I slide.

Words whisper in my ear, but I'm too far down here to understand them.

The dark mist is comforting. It beckons me to join and never leave.

I swear, there's a hint of warmth, just briefly. Soft lips tasting of guilt and love.

But I'm so far down here, and the dark cloak of death wraps around me, claiming me.

CHAPTER 22

BURNING.

Burning, burning, burning.

I lie in a vat of bubbling, boiling acid. It seeps into my skin. It eats through it, through every nerve, every muscle. Right down to my bones.

Everything that makes me a person boils and sizzles away as I burn and burn and burn.

Silently, I scream. Motionless, I writhe in pain and agony.

Dead, my heart lies dead in my chest. My lungs rest, entirely still. But my brain rages with infinite minutes of pain.

The seconds leading up to my death were terrifying and painful. But they were nothing compared to this.

This.

Resurrection. Cyrus' voice cuts through my brain, over and over again. First death. Turn. Transformation.

Vampire.

Born.

Royal.

Immortal.

One beat.

After a few lifetimes in hell, I feel it.

Another beat.

For the first time, something grabs at the edge of my brain, something beside the agony.

A vision. Of rolling green hills.

Another flash of sandstone buildings.

Another of a dark interior, stone walls.

And like floodgates opening, as I feel five consecutive beats inside my chest, *they* come rushing back.

Antoinette.

Helda.

Jafari.

Itsuko.

Edith.

Backward my brain spirals, searching, scrambling for the right one.

Deserts.

Jungles.

Mountains.

Each place to a name.

Each with a lifetime.

Shaku.

La'ei.

Searching, groping through the world, I desperately reach.

Until there.

Within the walls of a stone castle carved into the side of a mountain, I find it.

Thundering, my heart claims me. Forces me to accept this new life.

My eyes open.

And the name slips over my lips.

"Sevan."

THE END OF BOOK ONE

ABOUT THE AUTHOR

Keary Taylor is the USA TODAY best-selling author of over twenty novels. She grew up along the foothills of the Rocky Mountains where she started creating imaginary worlds and daring characters who always fell in love. She  now splits her time between a tiny island in the Pacific Northwest and Utah, dragging along her husband and their two children. She continues to have an overactive imagination that frequently keeps her up at night.

To learn more about Keary, please visit her website: www.kearytaylor.com.

Made in United States
North Haven, CT
18 March 2024